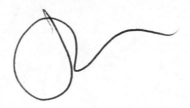

Samad Behrangi

Samad Behrangi (1939-1968) was born in Tabriz, the commercial and administrative center of Azarbayjan province, Iran. In 1957 he began to teach in the rural villages of his natal province and was soon forced to face the knowledge that the books and methods were long outdated or otherwise inappropriate to the village children. Moreover, his strong social sense of injustice and hatred of sham and arrogance led him inevitably to attempt to create a body of work which would touch the lives of children immediately and to bridge the inhuman gap between the rural poor and the better-placed townpeople and rich land-owners. He urged readers to learn about the lives of all Iranians by visiting "villages and towns" and to associate with "all kinds of people."

His short stories, five of which are translated in this collection, deal with powerless individuals, especially children, who not only share the poverty of their parents, but must struggle to survive physically and mentally in a society which has long ignored their vulnerable natures. His style and vocabulary, innovations in themselves, reflect everyday speech. And because he did not believe that young people should be protected from knowledge of the harsh realities of life, he told stories with real pain, coarseness—and even cruelty.

His stories, then, are about and for children: they are also thinly-coded protests against mass poverty and ignorance.

Behrangi died at age 29 while swimming in a swift Azarbayjan river. This, plus his warm-hearted qualities, his pioneering stories, and his strong social consciousness, have made him a central figure in contemporary Persian literature and culture. Except for the story "The Little Black Fish" which has appeared in a different translation in *The Literary Review* and in a second version in an "underground" translation, none of these stories have appeared in English.

The Little Black Fish
and Other
Modern Persian Stories

The Little Black Fish
and
Other Modern Persian Stories
by
Samad Behrangi

Translators: Eric Hooglund (The Little Black Fish), and Mary
Hooglund (24 Restless Hours; One Peach—A Thousand
Peaches; The Little Sugar Beet Vendor; The Bald Pigeon
Keeper.)

With a Bibliographical-Historical Essay by Thomas Ricks and an
English translation by Azad of "It's Night, Yes Night,"
Dr. Gholam Husayn Sa'edi's memorial essay on
Behrangi.

THREE CONTINENTS PRESS
Washington, D.C.

ISBN 0-914478-21-4 (Hardcover)
ISBN 0-914478-22-2 (Softcover)
Library of Congress Catalog Number: 75-42512

Cover design by Patty Zukerowski

Three Continents Press
4201 Cathedral Avenue, N.W.
Washington, D.C. 20016

To the memory of Fazel

"If someday I should be forced to face death — as I shall — it doesn't matter. What does matter is the influence that my life or death will have on the lives of others."

The Little Black Fish

Contents

Acknowledgments

We first became acquainted with and interested in the short stories of the late Samad Behrangi while spending the academic year 1971-72 studying in Iran. At that time Behrangi's works were enjoying widespread popularity in the country. The University of Tehran even sponsored a special Behrangi festival in the fall of 1971. However, since his writings generally express criticism of the social, political, and economic structures of contemporary Iran, Behrangi's stories have always been viewed with suspicion by leading members of the government. Thus, in 1973 all of Behrangi's writings, with the exception of the story of The Little Black Fish, *were officially banned by the branch of the security police in charge of censorship.*

Although Behrangi's stories are no longer available, except through private and underground sources, their place in Persian literature has been well-established. Behrangi certainly has become one of the most important writers of 20th century Iran. Yet, outside his own country his stories are virtually unknown. Even among the community of international scholars who study Iran there is little knowledge of Behrangi's works due to the difficulties in obtaining copies. Thus, a primary objective for this present collection of translations is to provide an introduction to Behrangi's short stories for both those who have special interests in Iran and those English readers who enjoy good literature.

This book would not have been possible without the assistance of many friends. The translation has particularly benefitted from the suggestions of several Iranian friends who shared both their time and knowledge of colloquial Persian. We are grateful to all who have helped in this important task, but especially wish to thank Azad, Khusheh, A. Mobarez, and Sogol. Each of the stories went through several drafts before reaching the final versions. Editing these various drafts was a tedious but necessary procedure and we are grateful to the help received from Margaret Goodman, Paul Haley, Karen Henderson-Dorman, Michael Hillman, Cynthia Mitchell, Louise Platt, and Thomas Ricks. The typing was also time consuming and thus Ruth Hegland deserves a tribute for her patience.

M. and E. Hooglund
Washington 1975

Translators'
Introduction

Samad Behrangi (1939-1968) was born in Tabriz, the commercial and administrative center of Azarbayjan province, Iran. He was educated in Tabriz and in 1957, after completing the two year program at the local Teachers' Training College, began teaching in the villages. His experience as a teacher in rural Azarbayjan had a crucial influence upon his writings which include critical essays about the education system, collections of folk tales, short stories based upon popular folk themes, and original stories which deal with various social aspects of village life and the problems of peasants who have migrated to the cities. During his eleven years as a teacher, Behrangi also travelled widely in Iran and earned a B.A. in English from Tabriz University. His untimely death occurred at age 29 when he drown while swimming with a friend in an Azarbayjan river.

Despite a short literary career, Behrangi's output was voluminous (see bibliography at the conclusion of Professor Ricks' essay). At the time of his death he was already recognized as one of the most important writers of contemporary Iran. The memorial essay by the playwright,

Gholam Husayn Sa'edi, attests to the extraordinary influence and respected status Behrangi had attained among Iranian artists and intellectuals, even though his most popular works belong to the genre of children's literature. Behrangi's reputation is based primarily upon his short stories which, although written originally for a youthful audience, contain social themes and philosophy of ageless appeal.

The short stories are a reflection of Behrangi's own life which was spent among ordinary people. Thus, his stories deal with powerless individuals, especially children, who must struggle with overwhelming political, social, and economic problems. His characters, settings, and situations are derived from familiar examples in Iranian society. His style is reflective of the everyday speech of the common people: simple sentences and colloquial vocabulary. All these features account for the widespread popularity of his stories in Iran. While Behrangi's short stories are written in the form of children's literature, they contrast sharply to the conventional types written for American children. Behrangi wrote realistic stories because he did not believe that young people should be protected from knowledge of the harsh realities of life. He believed that an early awareness of social problems was the best preparation for shouldering the responsibilities of improving society.

Behrangi's stories demonstrate the author's concern about the social and economic barriers between groups in Iran, the general ignorance among upper, middle, and lower classes about one another's lives, and the derogatory, stereotype views which townspeople and villagers held about each other. Behrangi tried to be a human bond between these groups. In his role as teacher he sought to impart to the villagers knowledge of a larger world. As a writer, he attempted to inform city dwellers about peasants. He tried to explain the economic deprivation which the rural poor suffer and to destroy common middle class myths and misconceptions about villagers. He urged readers to learn about the lives of all Iranians by visiting "villages and towns" and associating "with different kinds of people."

Behrangi believed that knowledge about society was a prerequisite for any action to correct social ills. Thus, his stories feature heros and heroines struggling against individuals, influences, and conditions which may be characterized as "evil". In *The Bald Pigeon Keeper,* for example, Kachel successfully combats a tyrannical establishment (the king and his chief minister) with the aid of his clever animals. However, the "battle" between Kachel and the forces of evil has no final victory. Instead, the conflict is permanent in nature. Kachel's continuing success depends upon a constant vigil and maintenance of a simple and humble lifestyle.

Thus, Behrangi did not view his stories as entertainment, but as a means to acquaint readers, as stated in his preface to *The Bald Pigeon Keeper,* "with our own society and with other nations and show them the troubles of society." Three of the five stories in this collection serve just this function while, at the same time, they offer the reader very original and moving stories. *One Peach—A Thousand Peaches* tells of two peasant boys who try to secretly grow their own peach tree in the walled orchard of a wealthy landlord. During the course of the story the reader learns about the poverty of villagers and the inequalities of land tenure. *The Little Sugar Beet Vendor,* which also has a village setting, deals with a very poor, but proud family which refuses to sacrifice its honor for the sake of monetary rewards. *24 Restless Hours* presents a glimpse into the lives of rural migrants trying to eke out a living in urban Tehran.

Behrangi emphasized two themes in his stories: (1) the acquisition of knowledge and (2) the use of knowledge to help correct social problems. These themes reach their fullest philosophical development in Behrangi's most important story, *The Little Black Fish*. This is an original tale about a fish who uses its "eyes, and ears and understanding" to learn about life as it encounters various societies while on a journey to find "the end of the stream." Once it travels the fish realizes that no group has a monopoly of knowledge: the larger societies of tadpoles and tiny fish are just as circumscribed in their world views as the smaller, isolated environment which the fish left behind in the stream; that individuals can be arrogant (the frog); crafty(the crab); opportunistic (the tiny fish); deceitful (the pelican); and dangerous (the heron); as well as kind (the lizard); wise (the moon); sensitive (the deer); and liberal-minded (the school of sea fish). The fish uses the knowledge gained from these accumulated experiences to formulate its own life view: to struggle throughout life against those who would deny experience and learning as means to throw off all types of personal and political oppression.

The Little Black Fish is the most important of Behrangi's works because its philosophy contains all of his essential ideas about society: that one should continually question his environment, oppose injustices, struggle against tyranny, work actively to change the ills of society. These ideas mark a sharp break with the themes typically found in earlier 20th century Iranian literature. Whereas previous contemporary writers (e.g., Sadiq Hidayat) described social problems with a heavy sense of despair and fatalism, Behrangi's writings are infused with a conviction that society can be improved through appropriate action. Above all, Behrangi believed that individual efforts could be effective, as exemplified by the little black fish.

The essential philosophy of *The Little Black Fish* has appealed to Iranians of all ages. Those who desire to effect certain political, social, and economic changes in their society have found this story especially relevant. Politically active groups claim Behrangi, or Samad as he is popularly known, as their hero and inspiration. The translation of the memorial speech which the writer and political dissident Gholam Husayn Sa 'edi presented at Behrangi's funeral presents some indication of the widespread influence of the latter.

Because *The Little Black Fish* has universal appeal as well as being significant to thoughtful Iranians, its story is similar in this respect to such internationally appreciated "children's stories" as Antoine De Saint-Exupery's *Le Petit Prince* and Richard Bach's *Jonathan Livingston Seagull.* It has already received critical acclaim outside of Iran. In 1969 *The Little Black Fish* won awards at international literature festivals in Bologna, Italy and Bratislava, Czechoslovakia. This international recognition has enhanced the story's prestige within Iran. Indeed, when Behrangi's works are periodically banned (as at present), *The Little Black Fish* is the only one of his writings which has escaped censorship.

The present translation of *The Little Black Fish* is not the first one in English. However, it is the first attempt to translate the story into colloquial English, avoid the turgidity of Persian phraseology, and at the same time remain as faithful as possible to Behrangi's original meaning. As is usually necessary when translating, certain liberties have been taken with literalness in order to avoid ambiguous passages. Readers will note that the fish has no specified gender. This was a deliberate choice of the translator. In Persian there is only a single pronoun which is used for he, she, or it. Normally, sex can be determined from the context. However, Behrangi avoids indicating the gender of the fish, although the sex of other animals often is obvious. The translator believes that Behrangi deliberately left the gender of the little black fish vague so that both boys and girls could readily identify with it. The translator has sought to preserve Behrangi's intent by substituting "the fish" in most instances where the Persian uses the neutral pronoun. At times when "the fish" would be awkward, the English pronoun "it" has been used.

The Little Black Fish and other stories selected for inclusion in this collection comprise a quintet which provides a representative sample of Behrangi's work. Even though each story is unique, common to all of them are certain themes which may be drawn upon in evaluating Behrangi as a writer. Nevertheless, the author is subject to various interpretations. For example, are his stories children's tales and nothing more; or do they serve to mirror social conditions; or are they a form of protest literature; or are they revolutionary in content? Critics espousing any or some combination of these interpretations, as well as other viewpoints, are numerous among those familiar with Behrangi's stories. The two essays in this book offer both an Iranian and an American perspective of Behrangi and his work.

Gholam Husayn Sa'edi in his essay "It's Night, Yes Night" emphasizes Behrangi's role as a creative writer of children's literature: "he received thousands of letters from children" upon the publication of each of his stories. But Sa' edi very obviously considers Behrangi as more than an author of children's tales. He praises the realism of his stories, and suggests that they, like Behrangi's life, protest the shortcomings of society. Thomas Ricks presents a different viewpoint of Behrangi. Examining the writer within the context of modern Persian literary history, Ricks concludes that Behrangi was a revolutionary artist advocating through his stories the necessity for radical social change.

The five stories in this book may not suffice to judge adequately the validity of either of these interpretations. But, at the very least they should stimulate interest in and discussion of Behrangi. The introduction of this important

Iranian writer to an international audience thus should contribute to evaluating his role in both Persian and world literature.

It's Night, Yes Night
by Gholam Husayn Sa'edi
translated by Azad

"Death could come upon me very easily now. But as long as I am able to live, I shouldn't go out to meet death. Of course, if someday I should be forced to face death—as I shall—it doesn't matter. What does matter is the influence that my life or death will have on the lives of others."

"The Little Black Fish" — Samad Behrangi

Oh woe and sorrow
All moons and all stars
In the grass only one flower has grown
Which cries out in thirst   *An Azarbayjan verse*

Samad Behrangi has neither a birthdate nor date of death. A biography would not do his life justice. His death is as unbelievable as was his life which was always so full of excitement that it resembled fiction. He was a teacher. Although he was exiled to the villages, he loved them. There was no distinction between him and the village masses. For years, wearing his black coat, he walked the roads from village to village. Everyone knew him.

"Samad's here." "Samad left." "Samad's gone to Yam." "Samad's gone to Akhirjan." When he was in the rural areas, he didn't act like a city person. He would start

xxiii

a class in a stable, school, village square or graveyard. And he took part in village life. Harvest, mourning ceremonies, Koran readings, mosques, weddings, he went everywhere. He took everything as it came. He wouldn't complain or allow himself to be depressed or unhappy. He didn't cherish golden desires. He touched, experienced and tasted everything. He accepted only those things which were tangible, perceivable, bitter or sweet, things that existed, things which could be experienced, understood, taught. This is why he wasn't drawn toward understanding undefinable human pains. He was never subject to such pains.

He knew hunger, he knew poverty, he knew disease and oppression. He realized that all of the first-grade reading books had no meaning for the peasants and that it was impossible to explain postal service, congratulatory cards, telephone, dinner table and strawberries to Azarbayjan villagers. He would throw out such concepts. He would bravely cross out all such words in the text books. As a result, he considered doing something about it himself, and he did. He wrote a first-grade reading book for the village children which had no parallel in Persian. Even the educational authorities liked it. But the publication of this reader was prohibited[by the government].He tucked his book under his arm and without a frown returned to the same little villages and broken-down huts.

All by himself, with the book he had written, he showed everyone how easy it is to learn to read and write. He firmly believed in the power of every language.

Therefore he worked very hard. He loved his mother tongue [Azari Turkish] more than one could imagine and was extremely skillful in reading and writing it. He wrote and published.

He was not afraid of problems. He was only surprised that he didn't have the right to publish in his mother tongue [Azari Turkish, the language spoken in Azarbayjan]. He was determined to collect Azarbayjan folklore and visited all little villages and isolated towns. Through his collection, he showed what strength there could be in a language.

At the same time he prepared a book of poems from this folklore, but once again publication was prevented. He decided to collect Azarbayjan folk tales, and with the cooperation of his closest friend, Behruz Dehqani, he fulfilled this ambition, then translated two volumes of the tales into Persian and published them.

But this was not his main task. He was gifted with a unique imagination and the ability to compose stories. He was always writing. His stories sometimes resembled local folk tales, for he believed he should write for everyone and therefore purposely chose characters for his stories which would be familiar to everyone.

He had unending patience for this work and for urging publishers to sell his books at low prices. In letters to friends or authors he would always argue that books were too expensive. He spent all of his money on books and on weekends and holidays would go to the villages with a bag of books and lend them out to everyone. Then he would sit and talk with everyone about books. Good books created a duty for him, the duty of taking them to the masses. They weren't aware or conscious, but he knew and was very conscious. In this way he became a traveling librarian in the villages of Azarbayjan.

As time went by he became more powerful in his story writing ability. The number of his published and unpublished books and articles in recent years is quite significant.

In his critiques he judged unmercifully. He wouldn't insult or ridicule. He didn't try to show off. He would only point out shortcomings.

He was extremely familiar with contemporary Iranian literature. He had such a command of the

Azarbayjan language that he translated the most difficult works of Nima Yushij, Ahmad Shamlu, Akhvan Sales, Farugh Farrokhzad and M. Azad into his mother tongue. He showed amazing attention to sound and rhythm in his choice of each word. He has left us a remarkable collection of his unpublished translations which will doubtlessly deeply influence the development of the Azarbayjan language.

But this was not his only accomplishment. His masterpiece was his life. He was constantly learning and teaching.

In his free time, he would go to the bookstores to advise the young people who came to buy books. Sometimes he would stand seriously in front of a customer who had chosen a worthless book and convince him to buy another book. He would walk around in public libraries looking at tables and start a discussion: "Don't read this." "This is trash." "Plenty of good books have been published," "Not every book should be read, not every book should be read, not every book should be read."

After the release of each of his books, he received thousands of letters from children, and he answered all of them. He had a rare patience for this task. His pockets were always full of letters children had written to him asking if it wouldn't be better if "Ulduz" had done such and such or wanting to know what was going to happen next.

No one can believe his death. And is Samad really dead? It's not possible. Samad's not dead, Samad is alive. Right now, he's on the way to Mameqan, talking with the children.

He's gone to Pakehjin. He's helping the fruit pickers in the villages around Maragheh. He's sitting and chatting with the old women of Ilkhchi. He's in the public library. He's watching the traveling showman behind the Golestan Garden. He's in the libraries. He's in the publishing houses editing another "Love Tale." No, it's a lie. Don't believe it. Samad isn't dead. Samad is alive, Samad is alive. Samad is alive.

Special Note on Gholam Husayn Sa'edi

"It's Night, Yes Night" is from the second printing of the special edition of the literary journal *Aresh, Darbareh-yi Samad-i Behrangi (Aresh, About Samad Behrangi),* Vol. 5, No. 18, Azar 1347/Nov.-Dec. 1968, pp. 15, 16, 106, 107. The author, Gholam Husayn Sa'edi, who was a close friend of Behrangi, is a prominent social critic and writer of plays and short stories, at least one of which has been translated into English. (See Sa'edi, Gholam Husayn, "The Wedding", translated by Jerome W. Clinton, *Iranian Studies, Journal of the Society for Iranian Studies,* Vol. VIII, Numbers 1-2, Winter-Spring, 1975, pp. 2-47). Sa'edi has been arrested many times and subjected to other types of harassment because of his literary works. He was last arrested May, 1974 and was later sentenced to thirteen years in prison. (*Le Monde,* Feb. 9-10, 1975, p.4). However, after apparently undergoing severe torture, he was released Spring, 1975. The June 19, 1975 issue of the government-controlled Tehran newspaper, *Kayhan,* published an interview with Sa'edi in which he reportedly repudiates his former writings and vows to write in the future about the accomplishments of the Shah's "White Revolution." (See *Kayhan,* Khordad 29, 1354/June 19, 1975, pp. 35, 39).

The Little Black Fish

It was the coldest night of the winter. At the bottom of the sea an old fish gathered together 12,000 of her children and grandchildren and began to tell them a story:

Once upon a time a little black fish lived with its mother in a stream which rose out of the rocky walls of a mountain and flowed through a valley. Their home was behind a black, moss-covered rock, under which both of them slept at night. The little fish longed to see the moonlight in their home just once.

From morning til evening, the mother and child swam after each other. Sometimes they joined other fish and rapidly darted in and out of small places. The little fish was an only child, for of the 10,000 eggs which the mother had laid, only this one had survived.

For several days the little fish had been deep in thought and said very little, but swam lazily and indifferently back and forth from the near to the far bank. Mostly, the fish lagged behind the mother who thought her child was sick and soon would be well. In fact, the black fish's "sickness" was really something else!

Early one morning before the sun had risen, the little

1

fish woke the mother and said, "Mother, I want to talk to you."

Half-asleep, the mother responded, "My dear child, this isn't the time to talk. Save your words for later. Wouldn't it be better to go swimming?"

"No, Mother! I can't go swimming anymore. I must leave here."

"Do you really have to leave?"

"Yes, Mother, I must go."

"Just a minute! Where do you want to go at this hour of the morning?"

"I want to go see where the stream ends. You know, Mother, for months I've been wondering where the end of the stream is . . . I haven't been able to think about anything else. I didn't sleep a wink all night. At last, I decided to go and find where the stream ends. I want to know what's happening in other places."

The mother laughed. "When I was a child, I used to think a lot like that. But, my dear, a stream has no beginning and no end. That's the way it is. The stream just flows and never goes anywhere."

"But Mother dear, isn't it true that everything comes to an end? Nights end, days end, weeks, months, years . . . "

"Forget this pretentious talk," interrupted the mother. "Let's go swimming. Now's the time to swim, not talk."

"No, Mother, I'm tired of this swimming. I want to set out and see what's happening elsewhere. Maybe you think someone taught me these ideas but believe me, I've had these thoughts for a long time. Of course, I've learned many things here and there. For instance, I know that when most fish get old, they complain about everything. I want to know if life is simply for circling around in a small place until you become old and nothing else, or is there another way to live in the world?"

When the little fish finished, the mother exclaimed: "My dear child, are you crazy? World! . . . World! What is this other world! The world is right here where we are. Life is just as we have it . . . "

Just then, a large fish approached their home and said: "Neighbor, what are you arguing about with your child? Aren't you planning to go swimming today?"

Hearing her neighbor's voice, the mother came out of the house and said, "What's the world coming to! Now children even want to teach their mothers something!"

"How so?" asked the neighbor.

"Listen to the places this half-pint wants to go!" replied the mother. "Saying over and over again I want to go see what's happening in the world. What pretentious talk!"

"Little one," said the neighbor, "let's see. Since when have you become a scholar and philosopher and not told us?"

"Madam," answered the little fish, "I don't know what you mean by 'scholar' and 'philosopher,' I've just gotten tired of these swims. I don't want to continue this boring stuff and be happy as a fool until one day I wake up and see that like all of you, I've become old, but still am as dumb as I am now."

"Oh, what talk!" exclaimed the neighbor.

"I never thought my only child would turn out this way," said the mother. "I don't know what evil person put my sweet baby up to this."

"No one put me up to anything," said the little fish. "I have reason, and intelligence and understanding. I have eyes and I can see."

"Sister," said the neighbor to the little fish's mother, "do you remember that twisted-up snail?"

"Yes, you're right," said the mother. "He used to push himself on my baby. God knows what I would do to him!"

3

"That's enough, Mother," said the little fish. "He was my friend."

"Friendship between a fish and a snail," said the mother, "I've never heard of such a thing!"

"And I've never heard of a fish and a snail being enemies," replied the little fish. "But you all drowned that poor fellow."

"Let's not bring up the past," said the neighbor.

"You brought up the subject yourself," said the little fish.

"It served him right to be killed," said the mother. "Have you forgotten the things he used to say everywhere he went?"

"Then," said the little fish, "kill me too since I'm saying the very same things."

To make a long story short, the arguing voices attracted the other fish. The little fish's words angered everyone. One of the old fish asked, "Did you think we'd pity you?"

"That one just needs a little box on the ears," said another.

"Go away," said the black fish's mother. "Don't you touch my child."

Another of them said, "Madam, if you don't raise your child correctly, you must expect it to be punished."

The neighbor said, "I'm ashamed to live next to you."

Another said, "Let's do to the little fish what we did to the old snail before it gets into trouble."

When they tried to grab the little black fish, its friends gathered around and took the fish away from the brawl. The black fish's mother beat her head and chest and cried, "Oh, my baby is leaving me. What am I going to do? What a curse has fallen upon me!"

"Mother, don't cry for me. Cry for the old fish who stay behind."

"Don't get smart, half-pint!" shouted one of the fish from afar.

"If you go away and afterwards regret it, we won't let you come back," said a second.

"These are youthful fancies. Don't go," said a third.

"What's wrong with this place?" said a fourth.

"There is no other world. The world is right here. Come back!" said a fifth.

"If you turn reasonable and come back, then we'll believe you really are an intelligent fish," said a sixth.

"Wait, we've gotten used to having you around . . . " said a seventh.

The mother cried, "Have mercy on me. Don't go! Don't go!"

The little fish didn't have anything more to say to them. Several friends of the same age accompanied the fish as far as the waterfall. As they parted, the fish said, "My friends, I hope to see you again. Don't forget me!"

"How would it be possible to forget you?" asked the friends. "You've awakened us from a deep sleep. You've taught us many things that we had not even thought about before. We hope to see you again, learned and fearless friend."

The little fish swam down the waterfall and fell into a pond full of water. At first the fish lost its balance but after a while began to swim and circled around the pond. The fish had never seen so much water collected in one place. Thousands of tadpoles were wriggling in the water. They laughed when they saw the little black fish, "What a funny shape! What kind of creature are you?"

The fish looked them over thoroughly and said, "Please don't insult me. My name is Little Black Fish. Tell me your names so that we'll get acquainted."

"We call one another tadpole," replied one of the tadpoles.

"We come from nobility," said another.

"You can't find anyone prettier than us in the whole world," said another.

"We aren't shapeless and ugly-faced like you," said another one.

The fish said, "I never imagined you would be so conceited. That's all right. I'll forgive you since you're speaking out of ignorance."

In one voice the tadpoles demanded, "Are you saying we're stupid?"

"If you weren't ignorant," replied the fish, "you'd know that there are many others in the world who are pleased with their appearances. You don't even have names of your own."

The tadpoles became very angry. But since they knew the little fish spoke truthfully, they changed their tone and said, "Really, you're wasting words! We swim around the world every day from morning til evening, but except for ourselves and our father and mother, we see no one. Of course, there are the tiny worms, but they don't count."

"You can't even leave the pond," said the fish. "How can you talk about traveling around the world?"

"What! Do you think there's a world other than the pond?" exclaimed the tadpoles.

"At least," responded the fish, "you must wonder where this water comes from and what things are outside of it."

"Outside the water!" exclaimed the tadpoles, "Where is that? We're never seen outside of the water! Haha .. .. haha . . . You're crazy!"

Little Black Fish also started to laugh. The fish thought it would be better to leave the tadpoles to themselves and go away, but then changed its mind and decided to speak to their mother.

"Where is your mother?" asked the fish.

Suddenly, the deep voice of a frog made the fish jump. The frog was sitting on a rock at the edge of the pond. She jumped into the water, came up to the fish and said:

"I'm right here. What do you want?"

"Hello, Great Lady," said the fish.

The frog responded "Worthless creature, now is not the time to show off. You've found some children to listen to you and are talking pretentiously. I've lived long enough to know that the world is this pond. Mind your own business and don't lead my children astray."

"If you lived a hundred years," said the little fish, "you'd still be nothing more than an ignorant and helpless frog."

The frog got angry and jumped at Little Black Fish. The fish flipped quickly and fled like lightening, stirring up sediment and worms at the bottom of the pond.

The valley twisted and curved. The stream became deeper and wider. But if you looked down at the valley from the top of the mountains, the stream would seem like a white thread. In one place, a piece of large rock had broken off from the mountain, fallen to the bottom of the valley, and split the water into two branches. A large lizard the size of a hand, lay on her stomach on the rock. She was enjoying the sun's warmth and watching a large, round crab resting on the sand at the bottom of the water in a shallow place and eating a frog he had snared. The little fish suddenly saw the crab, became frightened, and greeted him from afar. The crab glanced sideways at the fish and said, "What a polite fish! Come closer, little one. Come on!"

"I'm off to see the world," said the little fish, "and I never want to be caught by you, sir!"

"Little fish, why are you so pessimistic and scared?" asked the crab.

"I'm neither pessimistic nor afraid," answered the fish. "I speak about everything I see and understand."

7

"Well, then," said the crab, "please tell me what you've seen and understood that makes you think I want to capture you?"

"Don't try to trick me!" responded the fish.

"Are you referring to the frog?" queried the crab. "How childish you are! I have a grudge against frogs; that's the reason I hunt them. Do you know, they think they're the only creatures in the world and that they're very lucky. I want to make them understand who is really master in the world! So you don't have to be afraid, my dear. Come here. Come on."

As the crab talked, he was walking backwards towards the little fish. His gait was so funny that the fish couldn't help laughing and said, "Poor thing! You don't even know how to walk. How did you ever learn who runs the world?"

The black fish drew back from the crab. A shadow fell upon the water and suddenly a heavy blow pushed the crab into the sand. The lizard laughed so hard at the crab's expression that she slipped and almost fell into the water. The crab couldn't get up. The little fish saw that a young shepherd was standing at the edge of the water watching the fish and the crab. A flock of sheep and goats came up to the water and thrust their mouths in. The valley filled with the sounds of "meh meh" and "bah bah."

The little black fish waited until the sheep and goats had drunk their water and left, then called the lizard, "Dear lizard, I'm a little black fish who's going to search for the end of the stream. I think you're wise, so, I'd like to ask you something."

"Ask anything you want."

"All along the way, they've been frightening me a great deal about the pelican, the swordfish and the heron. Do you know anything about them?"

"The swordfish and the heron," said the lizard, "aren't found in this area, especially the swordfish who

8

lives in the sea. But it's possible that the pelican is farther down. Be careful he doesn't trick you and catch you in his pouch."

"What pouch?"

"Under his throat," explained the lizard, "the pelican has a pouch which holds a lot of water. When the pelican's swimming, fish, without realizing it, sometimes enter his pouch and then go straight into his stomach. But if the pelican isn't hungry, he stores the fish in his pouch to eat later."

"If a fish enters the pouch, is there any way of getting out?" asked the fish.

"There's no way unless the fish rips open the pouch," answered the lizard. "I'm going to give you a dagger so that if you get caught by the pelican, you can do just that."

Then the lizard crawled into a crack in the rock and returned with a very sharp dagger. The little fish took the dagger and said, "Dear lizard, you are so kind! I don't know how to thank you."

"It's not necessary to thank me, my dear. I have many of these daggers. When I have nothing to do, I sit down and make daggers from blades of grass and give them to smart fish like you."

"What?" asked the fish, "Have other fish passed here before me?"

"Many have passed by," the lizard replied. "They've formed themselves into a school and they give the fisherman a hard time."

"Excuse me for talking so much," said the black fish, "but if you don't think me meddlesome, tell me how they give the fisherman a hard time."

"Well," answered the lizard, "they stick together. Whenever the fisherman throws his net, they get inside, pull the net with them, and drag it to the bottom of the sea."

9

The lizard placed her ear on the crack, listened and said, "I must excuse myself now. My children have awakened."

The lizard went into the crack in the rock. The black fish had no choice but to set out again. But all the while there were many questions on the fish's mind. "Is it true that the stream flows to the sea? If only the pelican doesn't catch me! Is it true the swordfish enjoys killing and eating its own kind? Why is the heron our enemy?"

The little fish continued swimming and thinking. In every stretch of the way the fish saw and learned new things. How the fish liked turning sommersaults, tumbling down waterfalls, and swimming again! The fish felt the warmth of the sun and grew strong. At one place a deer was hastily drinking some water. The little fish greeted her. "Pretty deer, why are you in such a hurry?"

"A hunter is following me," replied the deer. "I've been hit by a bullet. . . . right here!"

The little fish didn't see the bullet hole, but from the deer's limping gait knew she was telling the truth.

At one place turtles were napping in the sun's warmth. At another place the boisterous noise of partridges twisted through the valley. The fragrance of mountain grass floated through the air and mixed with the water.

In the afternoon the fish reached a spot where the valley widened and the water passed through the center of a grove of trees. There was so much water that the little black fish had a really good time. Later on the fish came upon a school of fish. The little fish had not seen any other fish since leaving home. Several tiny fish surrounded Little Black Fish and said, "You must be a stranger here!"

"Yes," responded the black fish, "I'm a stranger. I've come from far away."

"Where do you want to go?" asked the tiny fish.

"I'm going to find the end of the stream," replied the black fish.

"Which stream?"

"This very stream we're swimming in," answered the black fish.

"We call this a river," stated the tiny fish. The black fish didn't say anything.

"Don't you know that the pelican lives along the way?" inquired one of the tiny fish.

"Yes, I know," answered the black fish.

"Do you know what a big wide pouch the pelican has?" asked another.

"I know that too," replied the black fish.

"In spite of all this, you still want to go?" exclaimed the tiny fish.

"Yes," said the black fish, "whatever happens, I must go."

Soon a rumor spread among all the fish that a little black fish had come from far away and wanted to find the end of the river. And the fish wasn't even afraid of the pelican! Several tiny fish were tempted to go with the black fish but didn't because they were afraid of the grown-ups. Others said, "If there weren't a pelican, we would come with you. We're afraid of the pelican's pouch."

A village was on the edge of the river. Village women and girls were washing dishes and clothes in the river. The little fish listened to their chatter for a while and watched the children bathing, then set off. The fish went on and on and on, still farther on, until night fell, then lay down under a rock to sleep.

The fish woke in the middle of the night and saw the moon shining into the water and lighting up everything. The little black fish liked the moon very much. On nights when the moon shone into the water, the fish longed to creep out from under the moss and speak with her. But Mother would always wake up, pull the fish under the moss, and make it go to sleep again.

The little fish looked up at the moon "Hello, my lovely moon!"

"Hello, Little Black Fish. What brings you here?"

"I'm traveling around the world."

"The world is very big," said the moon. "You can't travel everywhere."

"That's okay," said the fish. "I'll go everywhere I can."

"I'd like to stay with you til morning," said the moon, "but a big, black cloud is coming toward me to block out my light."

"Beautiful moon! I like your light so much. I wish you'd always shine on me."

"My dear fish, the truth is, I don't have any light of my own. The sun gives me light and I reflect it to the earth. Tell me, have you heard that humans want to fly up and land on me in a few years?"

"That's impossible," exclaimed the fish.

"It's a difficult task," said the moon, "but whatever they want, humans can. . . . " The moon couldn't finish her sentence. The dark cloud approached and covered her face. The night became dark again, and the black fish was alone. The fish looked at the darkness in surprise and amazement for several seconds, then crept under a rock and fell asleep.

The fish woke up early in the morning and saw overhead several tiny fish chattering. When they saw that the black fish was awake, they said in one voice, "Good morning!"

The black fish recognized them right away and said, "Good morning! You followed me after all!"

"Yes," answered one of the tiny fish, "but we're still afraid."

"The thought of the pelican just won't go away," said another.

"You worry too much," said the black fish. "One shouldn't worry all the time. Let's start out and our fears will vanish completely."

But as they were about to set out, they felt the water all around them rise up and a lid was placed over them. It was dark everywhere and there was no way to escape. The black fish immediately realized that they had been caught in the pelican's pouch.

"My friends," said the little black fish, "we've been caught in the pelican's pouch, but there's a chance to escape."

All the tiny fish began to cry. One of them said, "There's no way to escape! It's your fault since you influenced us and led us astray."

"Now he's going to swallow us all, and then we'll die," said another.

Suddenly the sound of frightening laughter twisted through the water. It was the pelican. He kept on laughing and said, "What tiny fish I've caught! Haha. Haha. Truly, my heart bleeds for you. I don't want to swallow you! Haha. Haha . . . "

The tiny fish began pleading, "Your Excellency, Mr. Pelican! We've been hearing about you for a long time. If you'd be so kind as to open your distinguished beak a little so that we might go out, we'll always be grateful to you."

"I don't want to swallow you right now," said the pelican. "I've some fish stored. Look below."

Several large and tiny fish were scattered on the bottom of the pouch.

"Your Excellency, Mr. Pelican!" cried the tiny fish, "we haven't done anything. We're innocent. This little black fish led us astray . . . "

"Cowards!" exclaimed the little black fish, "are you

crying like this because you think this dishonest bird is merciful?"

"You don't know what you're saying," said the tiny fish. "Just wait and see . . . His Excellency, Mr. Pelican, will pardon us and swallow you!"

"Of course I'll pardon you," said the pelican. "But on one condition."

"Your condition, please, sir!" begged the tiny fish.

"Strangle that meddlesome fish, and then you'll get your freedom."

The little black fish moved aside and said to the tiny fish, "Don't agree! This deceitful bird wants to turn us against each other. I have a plan . . . "

But the tiny fish were so intent on saving themselves that they couldn't think of anything else. They advanced towards the little black fish who was sitting near the back of the pouch and talking slowly. "Cowards! Whatever happens, you've been caught and don't have a way to escape. And you're not strong enough to hurt me."

"We must strangle you," said the tiny fish. "We want freedom!"

"You've lost your senses," said the black fish. "Even if you strangle me, you won't escape. Don't fall for his tricks . . . "

"You're talking like this just to save youself," said the tiny fish. "Otherwise you wouldn't think of us at all."

"Just listen," said the black fish, "and I'll explain. I'll pretend I'm dead. Then, we'll see whether or not the pelican will free you. If you don't agree to this, I'll kill all of you with this dagger or rip open the pouch and escape while you . . ."

"Enough!" interrupted one of the fish. "I can't stand this talk. Oh, wee . . .oh, wee . . .oh, wee . . . "

"Why did you ever bring along this cry baby?" demanded the black fish upon seeing him cry. Then the

14

fish took out the dagger and held it in front of the tiny fish. Helpless, they agreed to the little fish's suggestion. They pretended to be fighting together. The black fish pretended to be dead. The others went forward and said, "Your Excellency, Mr. Pelican, we strangled the meddle-some black fish . . . "

"Good work!" laughed the pelican. "Now, as a reward, I'm going to swallow all of you alive so that you can have a nice stroll in my stomach!"

The tiny fish never had a chance. Quick as lightening they passed through the pelican's throat and were gone. But, at that very instant, the black fish drew the dagger, split open the wall of the pouch with one blow and fled. The pelican cried out in pain and smashed his head on the water, but he couldn't follow after the little fish.

The black fish went on and on and still farther on until it was noon. The river had passed through the mountains and valleys and now was flowing across a level plain. Several other smaller rivers had joined it from the right and the left, increasing its water greatly. The black fish was enjoying the immensity of the water. Soon the fish realized the water had no bottom. The fish swam this way and that way and didn't touch anywhere. There was so much water that the little fish got lost in it! No matter how far the fish swam, still the water was endless.

Suddenly, the fish noticed a large, long creature charging forward like lightening. There was a two-edged sword in front of its mouth. The little fish thought, "The swordfish! He's going to cut me to pieces this very instant!" Quickly the fish jumped out of the way and swam to the surface. After a while the fish went under the water again to look for the bottom. On the way the fish met a school of fish—thousands and thousands of fish.

"Friend," said the fish to one of them, "I'm a stranger. I've come from far away. Where is this place?"

The fish called his friends and said, "Look! An-

15

other . . ." Then replied to the black fish, "Friend, welcome to the sea."

Another said, "All rivers and streams flow here, except some which flow into swamps."

"You can join our group anytime you wish," said one of the fish.

The little black fish was happy to have reached the sea and said, "I'd like to travel around first, then I'll come join your group. I'd like to be with you the next time you pull down the fisherman's net."

"You'll get your wish soon," answered one of the fish. "Now go explore. But if you swim to the surface, watch out for the heron who isn't afraid of anyone these days. She doesn't stop bothering us til she's caught four or five fish a day."

The black fish then left the group of sea fish and began swimming. A little later the fish came to the surface of the sea. A warm sun was shining. The little black fish enjoyed feeling the sun's bright rays on its back. Calm and happy, the fish was swimming on the surface of the sea and thinking, "Death could come upon me very easily now. But as long as I'm able to live, I shouldn't go out to meet death. Of course, if someday I should be forced to face death—as I shall—it doesn't matter. What does matter is the influence that my life or death will have on the lives of others . . . "

The little black fish wasn't able to pursue these thoughts. A heron dived down, swooped up the fish, and carried it off. Caught in the heron's long beak, the little fish kicked and waved but couldn't get free. The heron had grabbed the fish's waist so tightly that its life was ebbing away. After all, how long can a little fish stay alive out of water? "If only the heron would swallow me this very instant," thought the fish, "then the water and moisture inside her stomach would prevent my death at least for a few minutes."

The fish addressed the heron with this thought in mind. "Why don't you swallow me alive? I'm one of those fish whose body becomes full of poison after death."

The heron didn't reply. She thought, "Oh, a tricky one! What are you up to? You want to get me talking so you can escape!"

Dry land was visible in the distance. It got closer and closer. "If we reach dry land," thought the fish, "all is finished."

"I know you want to take me to your children," said the fish, "but by the time we reach land, I'll be dead, and my body will become a sack full of poison. Why don't you have pity for your children?"

"Precaution is also a virtue!" thought the heron. "I can eat you myself and catch another fish for my children. . . . but let's see . . .could this be a trick? No, you can't do anything."

As the heron thought she noticed that the black fish's body was limp and motionless. "Does this mean you're dead," thought the heron. "Now I can't even eat you! I've ruined such a soft and delicate fish for no reason at all!"

"Hey, little one!" she called to the black fish. "Are you still half alive so that I can eat you?"

But she didn't finish speaking because the moment she opened her beak, the black fish jumped and fell down. The heron realized how badly she'd been tricked and dived after the little black fish. The fish streaked through the air like lightening. The fish had lost its senses from thirst for sea water and thrust its dry mouth into the moist wind of the sea. But as soon as the fish splashed into the water and took a new breath, the heron caught up and this time swallowed the fish so fast that the fish didn't understand what had happened. The fish only sensed that everywhere was wet and dark. There was no way out. The sound of crying could be heard. When the fish's eyes had become accustomed to the dark, it saw a tiny fish crouched in a

17

corner, crying. He wanted his mother. The black fish approached and said:

"Little one! . . .Get up! Think about what we should do. What are you crying for? Why do you want your mother?"

"You there . . .Who are you?" responded the tiny fish. "Can't you see? . . . I'm . . .dy . . .ing. O, me . . . oh, my . . .oh, oh . . .mama . . . I . . .I can't come with you to pull the fisherman's net to the bottom of the sea any more . . . oh, oh . . . oh, oh!"

"Enough, there!" said the little fish. "You'll disgrace all fish."

After the tiny fish had controlled his crying, the little fish continued, "I want to kill the heron and give peace of mind to all fish. But first, I must send you outside so that you don't ruin everything."

"You're dying yourself," replied the tiny fish. "How can you kill the heron?"

The little fish showed the dagger. "From right inside here, I'm going to rip open her stomach. Now listen to what I say. I'm going to start tossing back and forth in order to tickle the heron. As soon as she opens her mouth and begins to laugh, you jump out."

"Then what about you?" asked the tiny fish.

"Don't worry about me. I'm not coming out until I've killed this good-for-nothing."

The black fish stopped talking and began tossing back and forth and tickling the heron's stomach. The tiny fish was standing ready at the entrance of the heron's stomach. As soon as the heron opened her mouth and began to laugh, the tiny fish jumped out and fell into the water. But, no matter how long he waited, there wasn't any sign of the black fish. Suddenly, he saw the heron twist and turn and cry out. Then she began to beat her wings and fell down. She splashed into the water. She beat her wings again, then all movement stopped. But there was no sign of

Little Black Fish, and since that time, nothing has been heard.

The old fish finished her tale and said to her 12,000 children and grandchildren, "Now it's time to sleep, children. Go to bed."

"Grandmother!" exclaimed the children and grand-children, "You didn't say what happened to that tiny fish."

"We'll leave that for tomorrow night," said the old fish. "Now, it's time for bed. Goodnight."

Eleven thousand, nine hundred and ninety-nine little fish said goodnight and went to sleep. The grandmother fell asleep too. But try as she might, a little red fish couldn't get to sleep. All night long she thought about the sea . . . .

24 Restless Hours

Dear Readers,
I didn't write the story "24 Restless Hours" to set an example for you. My purpose is rather that you become better acquainted with your fellow children and think about a solution to their problems.

Samad Behrangi

If I were to write everything that happened to me in Tehran, it would take several volumes and perhaps be dull. Therefore I will recount only the last twenty-four hours which shouldn't be so tiresome. Of course I must also tell you how it happened that my father and I came to Tehran.

My father had been out of work for several months. Finally he and I left my mother, sister and brothers at home and went to Tehran in hopes of finding others from our home town who had been able to find work there. One acquaintance had an ice stand. Another bought and sold used clothing, and a third was an orange vendor.

My father also managed to obtain a hand cart and become a vendor. He hawked onions, potatoes, cucumbers

21

and other vegetables, earning enough to provide us with a bit of food and send something home to my mother as well. Sometimes I accompanied my father on his rounds, and sometimes I hung around the streets by myself, returning to my father only at night. Once in a while I sold wrapped rial chewing gum, charms and other such things.

Now let's get on with the story of my last twenty-four hours in Tehran. That night, Qasem, Ahmad Husayn, and the son of Zivar the lottery ticket vendor, and I were there as well as two others who had become our friends an hour earlier in front of the bank.

We four had been sitting on the steps in front of the bank discussing where to go to throw dice when the two newcomers came and sat beside us. Both of them were bigger than we were. One had a blind eye. The other was wearing new black shoes, but one dirty knee stuck out of a hole in his pants. Those two were worse off than we were.

The four of us began stealing glances at the new shoes. Then we eyed the fellow's face as well. Looking at each other, we boys whispered: "Friends, be careful, for we're at the side of a shoe thief."

The fellow noticed our stares and demanded, "What's the matter? Haven't you ever worn shoes before?"

"Leave'em alone, Mahmud," said his friend. "Don't you see their navels and asses sticking out? The poor things, how could they buy shoes?"

"You're right, that was a stupid question," Mahmud agreed. "I'm looking at their bare feet and yet I ask them if they haven't ever worn shoes."

His friend with the blind eye said, "Not everyone has a rich papa like yours who spends money like sand buying new shoes for his kid."

Both of them fell into a fit of laughter. We four were completely baffled. Ahmad Husayn looked at Zivar's boy. They both looked at Qasem. Then the three of them looked at me: "What shall we do? Get rid of them or let them go on hooting with laughter and making fun of us?"

"You thief!" I challenged Mahmud, "You stole the shoes!"

They both burst out laughing. Cheslim Kureh (Blind Eye) poked his buddy in the side with his elbow and kept saying, "Didn't I say so, Mahmud? . . .Ha ha! . . .Didn't I say so? . . .Heh heh . . .Heh . . .Heh! . . ."

Cars of all colors were parked along the street, so tightly packed that there seemed to be a steel wall stretched before us. Then a red car right in front of me started up, opening a space so I could see into the street.

All kinds of vehicles — taxis, cars, buses — jammed the street and slowly moved along bumper to bumper, making a lot of noise and generating confusion. They seemed to be shoving each other and shouting at one another. I think Tehran is the most crowded spot on earth and this street the most crowded in Tehran.

Cheshm Kureh and his friend were about to faint from laughter. I wished to god we'd get into a fight. I'd learned a new swear word and wanted to try it out, given even the slightest excuse. I wished Mahmud would slap me. Then I could get angry and say to him, "You hit me? I'll cut off your balls with a knife! Yeh, me!" With this in mind, I grabbed Mahmud by the collar and shouted, "If you're not a thief, then who bought the shoes for you?"

This time they stopped laughing. Mahmud quickly jerked free and said, "Sit down, kid. You don't know what you're talking about."

Cheshm Kureh separated us saying, "Let him go, Mahmud. You don't want to start a fight at this time of night. Let's enjoy the fun while it lasts."

The four of us still wanted to beat them up but Mahmud and Cheshm Kureh just wanted to joke around and have a few laughs.

"Look, Brother," Mahmud told me, "we don't want to get into a fight tonight. If you want a fight, let it wait til tomorrow night." And Cheshm Kureh said, "Tonight we just want to talk and laugh a little. Okay?"

"All right," I said.

A shiny automobile stopped across from us and parked in an empty space. A man, a woman, a little boy and a fluffy white poodle stepped out. The little boy was exactly the same height as Ahmad Husayn and was wearing shorts, white socks and two-tone sandals. His hair was combed and oiled. In one hand he held a pair of white-rimmed sunglasses, and his other hand was clasped in his father's. The woman, with bare arms and legs and wearing high heeled shoes, was holding the puppy's leash. As she passed, we smelled lovely perfume. Qasem picked up a nut shell at his feet and threw it hard at the back of the little boy's head. The little boy came back, looked at us and said, "Bums!"

"Get lost, sissy!" spit out Ahmad Husayn angrily.

I seized the opportunity to say, "I'm going to cut off your balls with a knife."

The others all burst into laughter. The father took the little boy's hand, and they entered a hotel a few meters up the street.

Again all eyes turned towards Mahmud's new shoes. "Shoes aren't really so important to me," said Mahmud amicably. "If you want, you can have them." Then he turned to Ahmad Husayn and said, "Come here, shorty. Come on, take off the shoes and put them on your own feet."

Ahmad Husayn threw a suspicious look at Mahmud's feet and didn't move. "Why do you stand and stare?" Mahmud asked. "Don't you want the shoes? Well, come and get them."

This time Ahmad Husayn stood up, went over to Mahmud, and bent down to take off the shoes. We three looked on without saying anything. Ahmad Husayn took a firm grip on Mahmud's foot and tugged, but his hands slipped, and he fell back on the sidewalk. Mahmud and Cheshm Kureh broke out into such laughter that I was sure their stomachs would start aching. Ahmad Husayn's hands were black. Cheshm Kureh kept poking Mahmud and saying, "Didn't I say so, Mahmud! . . .Ha, ha . . .Ha! . . . Didn't I say so? . . .Heh, heh . . .!"

You could see where Ahmad Husayn's fingers had slipped on Mahmud's foot. The three of us finally realized we'd been tricked. The laughter of those two jokers was contagious; we burst out laughing too. Ahmad Husayn resentfully got up off the sidewalk, looked at us a minute, and then he started to laugh too. We laughed as if we'd never stop! Passersby stared at us then moved on. I leaned over and examined Mahmud's foot closely — there wasn't any shoe! Mahmud had merely painted his feet to look like he was wearing new black shoes. It was quite a trick!

"Why don't we play dice," Mahmud suggested.

I had four rials. Qasem didn't say how much money he had. Our two new friends had five rials. Zivar's kid had ten rials. Ahmad Husayn had no money whatsoever. We went a ways down the street and began to throw dice in front of a closed shop, drawing straws to start the game. Zivar's son got the longest one. He threw the dice and got a five. Then Qasem threw and got a six. So he took a rial from Zivar's son and threw again. He got a two. He gave the dice to Mahmud who got a four. "This must be my lucky night!" shouted Mahmud, clapping his hands in glee and picking up two rials from Qasem. We threw the dice in pairs, like this, playing in succession.

When two well-dressed young men came along from the right, Ahmad Husayn ran forward and pleaded, "A rial . . . Sir, give me a rial . . . Come on! . . ." One of the men slapped Ahmad Husayn and shoved him aside. Ahmad Husayn ran in front of them and begged again, "Sir, give me a rial . . . A rial is nothing at all . . . Please . . ."

As they passed in front of us, the young man grabbed

Ahmad Husayn by the back of the neck, lifted him up, and put him on his stomach on the guard rail at the side of the street so his head hung towards the street and his feet towards the sidewalk. Ahmad Husayn flayed out his arms and legs until his feet reached the ground, then he stood up right there at the edge of the gutter. Two smiling young girls and a young boy approached from the left. The girls were wearing pretty colored short dresses and were walking on either side of the boy. Ahmad Husayn ran up and entreated one of the girls, "Miss, please give me a rial . . .I'm hungry . . .One rial is nothing at all . . . Please! . . .Miss, one rial! . . .!"

The girl didn't pay any attention. Ahmad Husayn begged again. This time she took some money from her purse and placed it in Ahmad Husayn's palm. He came back to us, smiling, and said, "I'll throw, too."

"Where's your money?" asked Zivar's son.

Ahmad Husayn opened his fist and showed us. A two rial coin was in the palm of his hand.

Qasem said, "So you've been begging again!" and was about to hit Ahmad Husayn when Mahmud grabbed his arm and stopped him. Ahmad Husayn didn't say anything, just made a place for himself and sat down. I stood up and said, "I don't throw dice with beggars."

Now I had just one rial. I had lost three of my four rials. Mahmud, who hadn't done so well either, said, "That's enough dice throwing. Let's play foot of the wall."

"Latif,'Qasem said to me, "Don't spoil the game with your blabbering. Who wants to throw?" he asked around.

"Throw all by yourself," said Cheshm Kureh. "We're going to play foot of the wall."

Zivar's son pointed at Qasem and said, "It's useless throwing dice with this fellow. He always gets five and six. Let's flip coins."

"Fine," said Ahmad Husayn.

"No," Mahmud said, "Foot of the wall."

The street was getting quiet. Several shops across from us had closed. To start out the game, each of us threw a rial from the edge of the gutter to the foot of the wall. The coins were still laying there when Ahmad Husayn yelled, "Cops!"

The cop, billy club in hand, was two or three steps away from us. Ahmad Husayn, Cheshm Kureh and I started running. Mahmud and Zivar's son were right behind us. Qasem was about to gather the money from the foot of the wall when the cop reached him. The cop whacked him with the billy club, but he got away. "Gambling bums!" the cop shouted after him. "Don't you have a home and family? Don't you have a mother and father?" He bent over to gather the rials and then went on.

After I passed the intersection, I was left alone. The rice and kabab shop on the other side of the street was closed. I was late. When the rice and kabab apprentice pulled the iron door down halfway, it was time to get back to my father. I hurried through the streets saying to myself, "By now, father has surely fallen asleep. I wish he would sit and wait for me . . .By now he's fallen asleep. And what about the toy store? It's closed by now too. Who buys toys at this time of night? . . .Of course they've crammed my camel into the store, locked the door, and gone away . . .I wish I could talk with my camel. I'm afraid she'll forget what we planned last night. If she doesn't come? . . .No. She'll come for sure. She herself said she'd come tonight and carry me off for a ride around Tehran. Camel riding is fun too, ah! . . ."

Suddenly a brake screeched, and I was flung into the air so hard that I thought I was being thrown into the next world. When I fell to the ground, I realized I'd been struck by a car in the middle of the street, but miraculously I wasn't hurt. I was rubbing my wrist when a woman stuck her head out of the car and shouted, "Well, get out of the way of the car! . . .You're not a statue after all."

I suddenly came to. A heavily made-up old woman was sitting behind the steering wheel. The huge, collared dog curled up at her side looked out and barked. Suddenly I felt that if I didn't do something immediately— like break all the glass on the car—I would burst from the force of my anger and never be able to move from this spot.

The old woman honked the horn once or twice and yelled again, "Are you deaf or something? . . .Get out of the way of the car! . . ."

One or two other cars passed around us. The old woman stuck her head out and was about to say something else when I spit in her face, swore at her several times, and then ran off.

When I had run a ways, I sat down on the step of a locked store. My heart was beating fast. The store had a door of iron grating. It was light inside. All kinds of shoes were in the show window. My father had said that even with our earnings from ten days work we couldn't buy a pair of shoes like that.

I leaned my head against the door and stretched out my legs. My wrist still hurt, and my stomach was gnawing. I remembered that I hadn't eaten anything. "Tonight I'll have to go to sleep hungry again," I said to myself. "I wish that my father could have saved something for me . . ."

Suddenly I remembered that tonight my camel was coming to carry me off on a tour. I jumped up and quickly went on my way. The toy store was closed, but I could hear the toys behind the iron grating. The freight train chugged and whistled. The big black bear was sitting behind the machine gun and seemed to be firing off one shell after another, frightening the beautiful, lovable dolls. The monkeys leaped from corner to corner and sometimes hung from the camel's tail until the camel cried out and told them to move on. A donkey with long ears gnashed his teeth and hee hawed. He let bear cubs and dolls climb on his back and carried them around with long strides. The

camel's ears were pointing towards the ticking wall clock
as if she had made an appointment with someone. Airplanes
and helicopters flew overhead. Tortoises dozed in their
shells. Mother dogs were nursing their puppies. A cat
stealthily removed eggs from the bottom of a basket.
Rabbits stared in surprise at the hunter in the cupboard
across from them. The black monkey put my harmonica,
which was always in the show window, to this thick lips
and drew out various pretty tones. Dolls were riding in cars
and buses. Tanks, rifles, pistols and machine guns were
rapidly firing off bullets and shells. White bunnies held
huge carrots between their paws and gnawed so that their
teeth showed up to their ears.

Most important was my camel, who'd upset everything if she tried to move. She was so big that there wasn't
room for her in the show window so she stood at the edge
of the sidewalk all day long and watched the people. Now
she was standing in the middle of the store jingling the
bells around her neck, chewing gum, and pointing her ears
in the direction of the ticking clock. Every now and then a
row of white haired baby camels cried out from the
cupboard, "Mama, if you go out, let us come too, okay?"

I wanted to have a word or two with my camel, but
no matter how loud I shouted, she didn't hear my voice. I
kicked the door several times, hoping that the others
would quiet down, but just at that moment, someone
seized me by the ear and said, "Are you crazy, kid? Get
out of here and go to sleep."

It was no time to stand around. I freed myself from
the cop and set off so I wouldn't be any later.

By the time I reached my father, the streets were all
quiet and deserted. Lone taxis passed by. My father was
sleeping on top of his hand cart in such a position that if I
wanted to sleep there too, I'd have to wake him up and get
him to move his legs. Other carts with people sleeping on
them were at the edge of the gutter or by the side of the

wall. Several people had fallen asleep on the ground. There was an intersection here where someone from our home town had an ice stand. I fell asleep as I stood there and slowly slumped down at the foot of our hand cart.

Jingle! . . .Jingle! . . .Jingle! . . .

"–Ahoy, Latif, where are you? Latif, why don't you answer me? Why don't you come down so we can go riding?"

Jingle! . . .Jingle! . . .Jingle! . . .

"–Latif, dear, don't you hear me? I'm your camel. I came so we could go riding around. Well, come get on and let's go."

As my camel reached the balcony, I got out of bed and jumped, landing on her back. I said laughingly, "I'm sitting on your back, so don't shout any more!"

The camel was happy to see me, too. She put some gum in her mouth, gave some to me as well, and we went on our way. After we had gone a ways, the camel said, "I brought your harmonica. Take it and play something for me."

I took my lovely harmonica from the camel and began to blow into it energetically. The camel accompanied my playing with the jingling of her many bells.

The camel turned her head towards me and asked, "Latif, have you eaten?"

"No," I said, "I didn't have money."

"Then let's first go and eat dinner."

At that very moment, a white rabbit jumped down from a tree and said, "Camel, dear, we're having dinner at the villa tonight. I'll tell them. You go on." The rabbit tossed the end of the carrot that it had been chewing on into the gutter and hopped away.

"Do you know what a villa is?" asked the camel.

"I think it means summer quarters."

"No," the camel said, "Not summer quarters. Millionaires build palaces and magnificent houses for themselves in places with pleasant climates so that whenever they feel like it, they can go there to rest and enjoy themselves. These houses are called villas. Villas have pools, fountains, large gardens and flower plots full of flowers. They have a troupe of gardeners, cooks, servants and maids. Some millionaires own several villas in foreign countries, Switzerland and France for example. Now we're going to one of the villas in north Tehran to shrug off the summer heat from our bodies."

The camel said this and suddenly seemed to grow wings. We flew up into the air like birds. Below my feet were pretty, clean houses. There wasn't any smell of smoke or filth in the air. The houses and alleys were so neat that I thought I was watching a movie. I asked the camel, "We're not leaving Tehran, are we?"

"What made you think that?"

"Well," I said, "out here, there's no smell whatsoever of smoke or filth. The houses are all large and pretty as a bouquet of flowers."

The camel smiled and said, "You're right, Latif, my boy. Tehran has two parts, each with its own characteristics. North and South. The North is clean, but the South is full of smoke, filth, dust and dirt, because all the wornout buses operate in that section. All the brick kilns are in that section, and the diesels and trucks come and go from there. Many of the streets in the South aren't paved; the dirty putrid water in the open sewage gutters of the north flows downhill to the South. In short, the South is where the poor, hungry people live, and the North is the area of the rich and powerful. Have you ever seen the ten story marble buildings in 'Hasirabad', 'Naziabad' and Hajj Abdol Mahmud Avenue? In these buildings are the elegant shops of the rich, who own luxurious automobiles and dogs worth several thousand tomans."

I said, "In the South, you don't see such things.

31

There, no one owns cars, but a lot of people have hand carts and sleep in dugouts."

I was so hungry that I thought the bottom of my stomach was turning into a hole.

Below our feet was a huge garden with colored lights, cool and full of freshness, flowers, and trees. A large fountain like a bouquet of flowers was in the center and several meters away was a goldfish pool surrounded by tables and chairs, flowers, and blossoms. Lots of different foods with intoxicating odours were arranged on the tables.

The camel said, "Let's go down. Dinner's ready."

"But where's the owner of the garden?"

"Don't worry about him," the camel said. "He's been tied up and stuck into the basement."

The camel landed on the colorful glazed tiles at the edge of the pool, and I jumped down. The rabbit was ready. He took my hand and led me to one of the tables. A little later the guests began arriving. Dolls by car, a group by plane and helicopter, the donkey with rapid strides, tortoises hanging from the tails of baby camels, leaping and somersaulting monkeys, and scampering rabbits arrived all at once. What strange noisy guests they were for a dinner whose smell alone made the mouth water: fried turkeys, chicken kabab, all kinds of rice dishes and stewed meats, and many, many other foods that I didn't even recognize. Big bowls of every kind of fruit you would want were set within easy reach.

The camel stood on the other side of the pool, motioned everyone to be quiet and said, "Welcome everyone, large and small. It's a pleasure to have you here, but I'd like to ask you if you know why and for whose sake we've planned this expensive dinner."

"For Latif. We wanted him to eat one stomachful of good food to cheer him up," said the donkey.

The bear from behind the machine gun said, "Well,

Latif comes to watch us so often that we—all of us—like him."

"That's right," agreed the leopard. "Just as Latif wants to own us, we want to belong to him."

The lion said, "Right. Children of millionaires get tired of us very quickly. Their fathers buy new toys for them every day so they play with their toys once or twice, and then get bored and abandon us so that we wear out and die."

I began to speak. "If all of you will belong to me, I promise you I'll never get tired of you. I'll always play with you and won't leave you alone."

The toys said in one voice, "We know. We know what you're like. But we can't belong to you. We're sold for a lot of money."

Then one of them said, "I don't think that even a month of your father's earnings would be enough to buy one of us."

The camel quieted them down again and continued, "Let's get back to the subject. Your comments are all correct, but we planned this gathering for the sake of something very important which you haven't mentioned."

I spoke up again, "I myself know why you brought me here. You wanted to say to me, 'See, not everyone goes to sleep hungry at the side of the street like you and your father."

Several men and women were sitting around the table eating very quickly. Apparently they were the servants and maids of the house. I began to eat, too, but there seemed to be a hole at the bottom of my stomach so that no matter how much I ate it wasn't enough, and my stomach kept on growling and gurgling. Like all those times when I am very hungry.

I thought, "I'm surely not dreaming that I'm still hungry?" I drew my hand across my eyes. Both lids were open. I said to myself, "Am I sleeping? No, I'm not. The

33

eyelids of a person who's sleeping are closed, and he doesn't see. Then why aren't I satisfied? Why do I feel my stomach gnawing?"

I had been walking around the building and touching the expensive stones in its walls. I didn't know where the dust and dirt was coming from, and something hit me right in the face. I was in the basement now so I thought that's why the air was dusty. On the first step dirt flew into my nose and mouth so violently that I sneezed: "Ha chew! . . ."

"What happened?" I asked myself. "Where am I?"

The street sweeper's broom passed right in front of me and brushed the dust and dirt from the sidewalk into my face.

I asked myself, "What happened? Where am I? I wasn't dreaming, was I? But I wasn't sleeping, and I saw my father's hand cart and heard the noise of taxis. Then my eyes fell on the buildings of the intersection area in the morning twilight. So I was awake. The street sweeper had swept past me but still was throwing up dust and dirt, making streaks on the sidewalk, and moving forward.

I said to myself, "So, all of that was a dream? No! . . .Yes, it was a dream. No! . . .No! . .No! . ."

The street sweeper came back and stared at me. My father bent over from the hand cart and asked, "Latif, are you sleeping?"

"No! . .No! . ."

"If you're not sleeping, why are you shouting?" my father asked. "Come up beside me." I went up. My father put his arm under my head but I didn't go to sleep. My stomach gnawed. My stomach was stuck right against my backbone. My father saw that I wasn't sleeping and said, "You were late last night and I was tired so I went to sleep early."

"Two cars had an accident, and I stood and watched.

That's why I was late." Then I said, "Father, camels can talk and fly . . ."

"No, they can't."

"Yes, you're right," I said, "They don't have wings."

"Son, what's the matter with you? Every morning when you wake up you talk about camels."

I was thinking about something else and said, "Being rich is a good thing, Father, isn't it? A person can eat anything he wants and have anything he wants. Isn't that right, Father."

"Don't be ungrateful, Son. God Himself knows well who to make rich and who to make penniless."

My father always said this.

When it was light, my father took his slippers from beneath his head and put them on his feet. Then we got down from the hand cart. My father said, "I wasn't able to sell potatoes yesterday. I still have more than half of them."

"You should have gotten something else."

My father didn't say anything. He unlocked the padlock on the cart and took out two full bags and emptied them on the hand cart. I lifted out the scale and weights and arranged them. Then we went on our way.

"We'll go eat some soup," said my father.

Every morning that my father said, "We'll go eat some soup," I knew he hadn't eaten dinner the night before.

The sweeper had streaked the sidewalk to the end of the street. We went in the direction of City Park. The old soup vendor was sitting at the edge of the gutter as always, his back towards the street and a caldron of soup simmering over a slow fire in front of him. Three customers, men and women, were sitting around eating their soup from aluminum bowls. There was a woman lottery ticket vendor who wore a ragged veil like Zivar the lottery ticket vendor. She was crouched over and had put her bunch of lottery tickets on her lap and covered her knees with her dirty veil.

My father greeted the old man and sat down. We gulped two small soups with some bread and got up again. My father gave me two rials and said to me, "I'm going to make the rounds. Come back here at noon, and we'll eat lunch together."

The first person I saw was Zivar's boy. He had blocked a man's path and was repeating, "Sir, buy a ticket. You'll probably be a winner. Come on, Sir, buy one."

The man forcefully freed himself from Zivar's boy and went on. Zivar's kid muttered several curses and was about to walk away when I called out to him, "You weren't able to dump it on him!"

"He was in a bad mood; he's probably been fighting with his wife."

The two of us went on. Zivar's son stuck his bunch of ten or twenty tickets in front of people and repeated, "Sir, a lottery ticket? Madam, a lottery ticket?"

For every ticket that Zivar's boy sold, he got a rial from his mother. When he had covered his expenses, he didn't sell any more tickets but played, ran around, got into fights, or went to movies. He had more money than any of us. He had the habit of stretching out in the water gutter under the bridge at noon and sleeping for an hour or two. In the morning before the sun rose, he woke up and got ten or twenty lottery tickets from his mother and started on his way so that he wouldn't miss the morning customers and would finish his work before noon. He didn't want to ruin his afternoon as well by selling tickets.

Zivar's boy had sold three tickets by the time we reached Naderi Street. When we arrived there he said, "I have to stay right here."

Only a few stores were open. The toy store was closed. My camel hadn't come to the edge of the sidewalk yet. I didn't have the heart to pound on the door and disturb her morning sleep. I passed by and went farther and farther up the street. The streets were full of school children. In every car were one or two children whose parents were taking them to school.

At this time of morning I could only find Ahmad Husayn for company. After I passed through several more streets, I came to the streets where there wasn't any smoke or dirty smell. The children and adults all had clean fresh clothing. Their faces shone. The girls and women glowed just like colorful flowers. The stores and houses seemed like mirrors under the sun. Whenever I came to such areas, I thought I was sitting in a theater and watching a movie. I was never able to imagine what kind of food they ate, how they slept or spoke, or what kind of clothing they wore in such tall, clean houses. Can you figure out what kind of food you ate when you were in your mother's womb? No, you can't. I was like that. I couldn't imagine it at all.

Three children, satchels in hand, were looking into a store window. I stood behind them. A pleasant smell came from their combed hair. I couldn't help sniffing at the back of the neck of one of them. The children turned around, looked me over, moved away from me frowning in disgust, and left. From a distance I heard one of them say, "He sure smells!"

I had a chance to look at my reflection in the store window. My hair was so long and thick that it hid my ears. It looked like a hat of hair placed on my head. My burlap shirt was a dark dirty color and you could see my sun-burnt body at its torn collar. My bare feet were filthy, and my heels were cracked. I wanted to shatter the brains of the three rich children. But was it their fault that I lead such a life?

A man came out of the store, motioned me away and said, "Get out of here, kid. It's still early, and I haven't made any sales to give you something."

I didn't move and didn't say anything either. The

man motioned me away again and repeated, "Well, go on. Get lost. What impudence!"

I didn't move and said, "I'm not a beggar."

"Well, excuse me, Little Sir, then what do you want?"

"I don't want anything. I'm just looking."

And I left. The man went into the store. A piece of white glazed tile shone at the bottom of the water in the gutter. I didn't hesitate. I picked up the piece of tile and threw it with all my strength at the store window. There was a crash, and the glass broke into pieces. The shattering glass seemed to lift a heavy burden from my heart, and I started running as fast as I could! I don't know how many streets I had passed when I ran into Ahmad Husayn and realized I was now very far from the store.

As always, Ahmad Husayn was scurrying this way and that in front of the girls' school, begging at the cars that brought the girls. This is what Ahmad Husayn did every day early in the morning. I still don't know who Ahmad Husayn lived with, but Qasem said he had only a grandmother who was a beggar too. Ahmad Husayn himself never said anything.

When the school bell rang and the children went to class, we started on our way. Ahmad Husayn said, "I didn't bring much in today. Everyone says they don't have any change."

"Where shall we go?" I asked.

"Let's just wander around like this."

"No, that won't do, " I said. "Let's go and find Qasem and drink a glass of buttermilk."

Qasem sold rial glasses of buttermilk at the end of Si Metri Avenue, and everytime we went to see him, we drank a free glass of buttermilk. Qasem's father bought and sold used clothing on Hajj Abdol Mahmud Street; a shirt, fifteen rials; two pairs of shorts, twenty-five rials; coat and trousers, seventy or eighty rials. Hajj Abdol

Mahmud Street was one turn from the area where Qasem worked. Doorways, walls and even the ground of this street were littered with old dilapidated objects; each owner stood over his pile, calling to customers. Qasem's father had a tiny shop where he, his wife and Qasem, all three of them, also slept at night. They didn't have a house other than this. Qasem's father bought torn, dirty clothes from this one and that, and from morning to night, Qasem's mother washed them in the shop or in the gutter of Si Metri Street and then mended them. Hajj Abdol Mahmud Street was dusty and didn't have a water gutter. No vehicles passed through it.

After one or two hours of walking, Ahmad Husayn and I reached Qasem's work area. Qasem wasn't there, so we went to Hajj Abdol Mahmud Street. Qasem's father said that Qasem had taken his mother to the hospital. Qasem's mother was always having trouble with either aching legs or an ulcer.

Near noon, Ahmad Husayn, Zivar's boy and I were sitting at the edge of the gutter on Naderi Street next to the camel, cracking sunflower seeds and discussing the price of the camel. We decided to go inside and ask the storekeeper. The storekeeper thought we were beggars; we hadn't even gotten in the door when he ordered, "Get out of here. I don't have any change."

"We don't want money, Sir, " I objected. "How much is the camel?" And I pointed outside.

"The camel?!" the store owner asked in surprise.

From behind me Ahmad Husayn and Qasem repeated, "Yes, the camel. How much is it? "

The owner of the store said, "Go on outside! The camel's not for sale."

Discouraged, we left the store. As if we had enough cash to buy the camel anyway, even if it had been for sale. The camel was standing firmly in place. We imagined it could carry all three of us at the same time. without any effort whatsoever. Ahmad Husayn's hand could barely touch the camel's stomach. Qasem was about to try it when the storekeeper came out, seized Qasem's ear and said, "Ass, don't you see the sign says don't touch?"

And he pointed to a piece of paper pinned to the chest of the camel. Something was written on the paper, but none of us could read. We left and began walking and cracking sunflower seeds. A little later, Zivar's son said he was tired, found a quiet place in a water gutter under a bridge, and went to sleep. Ahmad Husayn and I decided to go to City Park. The air was hot and suffocating. We were sweating more than you could imagine. Neither of us spoke. I wanted to be with my mother. I felt very lonely.

At the City Park gate Ahmad spent two rials to buy an egg sandwich and let me take a bite too. Then we went to the usual spot in the water gutter to wash. Some other children were washing themselves farther up, splashing water on each other. Ahmad Husayn and I quietly stretched out in the water, washed our heads and bodies, and didn't bother anyone. The park guards came towards us shouting. We all jumped up to escape and went to sit on the sand under the sun. Ahmad Husayn and I were drawing a camel in the sand when I heard my father's voice over us. Ahmad Husayn went away. My father and I went to the liver shop and ate lunch. He asked, "Latif, what happened? Are you sick? "

"Nothing's happened."

We went under the trees of City Park and stretched out to sleep. My father noticed that I kept turning from side to side and couldn't sleep. "Latif, have you been fighting?" he asked. "Did someone insult you? Tell me what happened."

I didn't feel like talking. I wanted to grieve in silence. I wanted to hear my mother's voice, smell her, hug and kiss her. Suddenly I started crying and hid my face against my father's chest. My father sat up, held me, and let me cry as long as I wanted. But I still didn't say anything to him. I only said that I missed my mother. Then I fell asleep, and when my eyes opened, I saw my father sitting over me, his arms folded, looking into the crowd. I took his legs, shook them and said, "Father!"

My father looked at me, drew his hand over my hair and said, "Are you awake, my boy?" I nodded my head.

"Tomorrow we're going back home," my father said. "We're going to be with your mother. If there's work, we'll stay there and find something to eat. If there isn't, there isn't. Whatever happens it will be better than this, for here we're like worthless orphans. And the rest of the family is no better off without us."

On the way from the park to the garage, I didn't know whether to be happy or not. I didn't want to leave the camel. If only I could bring the camel with me, I wouldn't be unhappy anymore.

We bought our tickets, then started walking through the streets again. My father wanted somehow or another to sell his hand cart before evening. I wanted somehow or another to have one more long look at the camel. We planned to return to the garage at night to sleep. My father didn't want to leave me alone, but I said I wanted to walk around a while to shake off my depression.

It was near sunset. I don't know how many hours I had been standing and watching the camel when a convertible came by and stopped near me and the camel. A man and a fresh, clean little girl were sitting in the car. The girl's eyes were glued to the camel, and she was laughing happily, making me think they were going to buy the camel and take her home. The girl took her father's hand and got out of the car saying, "Faster, Daddy. Someone else will come and buy it."

The man and the girl were about to enter the store when they saw me standing in front of them, blocking the way. I don't know how I felt. Was I afraid? Was I about to cry? Was I unhappy about something? I don't know how I felt. I only know that I stood in front of the father and daughter and repeated, "Sir, the camel's not for sale."

The man pushed me roughly aside, saying, "Why are you blocking our path, kid? Get out of the way."

The two of them entered the store. The man began talking with the store owner. The girl turned back again and again to look at the camel. She looked so happy that you'd think she hadn't been even a bit sad in her whole life. My tongue seemed to be dumb and my legs powerless to move; I stood at the door and stared into the store. The monkeys, baby camels, bears, rabbits and the others looked at me, and I felt their hearts burning for me.

The father and daughter were about to come out of the store. The father stretched out a two rial coin towards me. I put my hands behind my back and looked into his face. I don't know what kind of look I gave him, but he quickly put the two rials into his pocket and passed by. Then the store owner pushed me away from the door. Two of the store workers came out and walked towards the camel. The little girl went and sat in the car and looked at the camel with worshipful eyes. When the store workers lifted up the camel, I didn't even think but ran forward and grabbed the leg of the camel, shouting, "This is my camel! Where are you taking it? I won't let you!"

One of the workers said, "Get out of the way, kid. Are you crazy or something?!"

The father asked the store owner, "Is he a beggar?"

People gathered to watch. I didn't let go of the camel's leg. The workers had to lower the camel to the ground and hold me back by force. I heard the voice of the girl calling from the car, "Daddy, don't let him touch it any more."

The father went and sat at the wheel. They put the camel in the back seat. The car was about to start up when I freed myself and ran towards it. I held on to the car with both hands and screamed, "Where are you taking my camel? I want my camel!"

I don't think anyone heard my voice. It was as if I had become dumb and no sound came from my throat and I only imagined I was screaming. The car started and someone grabbed me from behind. My hands were snatched from the car, and I fell on my face on the pavement. I lifted my head and saw my camel for the last time. She was crying and angrily ringing the bells around her neck.

My face fell in the blood running from my nose. I pounded my feet against the ground and sobbed. I only wished the machine gun in the store window belonged to me.

One Peach—A Thousand Peaches

At the edge of a poor, dusty village was a very large, well-watered orchard, full of different kinds of fruit trees. The orchard was so large and dense that if you looked from one side you couldn't see the other, even with binoculars.

Several years earlier, the owner of the village had divided most of his land into small plots and sold it to the peasants, but he kept the orchard for himself. Of course, the land he sold to the peasants was uneven and barren of trees. It didn't even have water. Originally, the village had included one level, arable piece of land in the middle of the valley—the landlord's orchard—and the stony land on hill tops and valley slopes which the villagers had now bought from the landlord and planted with wheat and barley, using dry farming techniques. Anyhow, enough of this chatter, since it probably doesn't have anything to do with our story.

Two peach trees grew in this orchard, one smaller and younger than the other. The leaves and blossoms of these two trees were so much alike that everybody at first glance realized they belonged to the same species.

45

The larger tree had been grafted and each year produced lovely, large, rosy peaches which would barely fit into your hand. They were almost too beautiful to eat. The gardener said a foreign expert had grafted the larger tree with stock brought from his own country. Obviously, peaches from such an expensively treated tree are quite valuable.

A charm was hanging around the trunk of each tree to ward off the evil eye.

The smaller peach tree put forth about a thousand blossoms every year but didn't produce one peach. Either its blossoms fell or the unripe peaches would wither and drop. The gardener did everything he could for the smaller tree, but there was no change. Year after year it grew more branches and leaves, but it never produced a peach.

The gardener decided to graft the smaller tree as well, but it still didn't change. You'd think it was being obstinate. Finally, the gardener was fed up. He wanted to play a trick and frighten the smaller tree. He went to fetch a saw, called his wife, and standing in front of the smaller peach tree began to sharpen the teeth of the saw. When the saw was sharp, he moved back and suddenly rushed towards the smaller peach tree as if he were going to saw it down right at the roots and throw it away so it wouldn't drop its peaches any more.

He was about to begin sawing when his wife grabbed his arm and said, "For my sake, don't saw it down! I swear that by next year, the little peach tree will produce fine, ripe fruit. If it's lazy again, then we'll both cut off its head and throw it in the oven to burn and turn to ashes." This threat didn't reform the tree either.

Of course, all of you want to know what the smaller peach tree had to say on its own behalf about why it didn't ripen its peaches. Very well. From here on the peach tree will tell the story.

* * *

Listen! . . .

Pay careful attention, for the smaller peach tree wants to talk. Don't make any noise—let's see what the smaller peach tree says. The tree describes its adventures like this:

We were a hundred or a hundred and fifty peaches sitting in a basket. The gardener had lined the top, bottom and sides of the basket with vine leaves so the sun wouldn't dry our delicate skins and dust wouldn't settle on our red cheeks. A bit of green light filtered through the thin vine leaves and was mixed with the red of our cheeks. It filled the heart with expectation.

The gardener had picked us early in the morning before the sun rose so our flesh was cool and moist. The chill of fall nights was still in our bodies, and the bit of warmth that passed through the green leaves clung to our hearts.

Of course, all of us were the children of one tree. Every year at this time, the gardener picked my mother's peaches, filled a basket, and took it to town. There, he went and knocked at the landlord's door, delivered the basket, and returned to the village. Just like now.

I was saying that we were a hundred, a hundred and fifty ripe, juicy peaches. I myself was full of sweet, delicious juice. You'd have thought my smooth, clear skin was about to burst. The red of my cheeks was so intense that if you had seen me, you would have thought that surely I was blushing from my own nakedness, especially since my head and sides were still wet from autumn dew as though I had just bathed.

My large, firm pit was thinking about a new life. Or rather, I should say that I myself was thinking about a new life as my pit was not separate from myself.

The gardener had put me at the top of the basket so that I would be seen at first glance, perhaps because I was larger and juicier than all the others. Of course, I'm not bragging about myself. All peaches who've had the opportunity to grow up and become big and ripe will be large and juicy, except those peaches who are careless and allow worms to enter their skin and flesh and to eat even their pits.

If we had reached the landlord sitting this way in the basket, I would have helplessly fallen to the hand of the landlord's dear only daughter who would have taken one bite out of my cheeks and thrown me away. For the landlord's house was not like the poor homes of Saheb Ali and Pulad where not one apricot, cucumber or peach ever came through the door. According to the gardener, the landlord imports fruit for his daughter from foreign countries. He orders oranges, bananas and grapes, even flowers brought for his daughter by plane. Of course, he spends money like sand to do this. Now calculate it yourself—how much money will it take for the clothes, school, food, doctor, nurse, servant, toys, trips and outings for the landlord's daughter? You say ten thousand tomans a month? No, that's not enough . . . But I'm getting off the subject.

The gardener, basket in hand, was walking along the path in the middle of the orchard when suddenly a mouse nest collapsed under his feet. The gardener almost fell but caught himself in time. The basket, though, was given a sharp jerk, and I slipped and fell on the dirt. The gardener didn't notice and went on.

By now, the sunshine had spread throughout the orchard. The ground felt warm, and the sunshine felt even warmer. Perhaps the sunshine seemed especially hot because my body was cool.

Little by little, the heat passed through my skin and into my flesh. My sap became warm. Then the heat reached my pit. In a little while I grew thirsty.

When I had been with my mother, whenever I got thirsty, I drank water from her. I would look at the sun so it would shine more on me and warm me. The sun would beam on me and make my cheeks feel hot. I sucked water from my mother, I ate food, and my sap flowed. Every day I grew larger and larger, prettier, rosier and juicier. More red ran in the veins of my face. I grew heavy and bent my mother's arm and swung.

My mother would say, "My beautiful daughter, don't hide yourself from the sunshine. The sun is our friend. The earth gives us food, and the sun cooks it. And your beauty is from the sun. See how pale and thin are the peaches who hide themselves from the sunshine. My beautiful daughter, you can be sure that if the sun should become angry with the earth some day and not shine on it, living things wouldn't remain on the earth, neither plants nor animals."

So I entrusted my body to the sunshine as much as I could, drew from its warmth, and stored it in myself. My strength increased day by day. I always asked myself:

"If someone should insult the sun some day and the sun should become angry with us, whatever would we do?" I was never able to find an answer, and I asked my mother, "Mother, if some day someone should insult Lady Sun and Lady Sun should become angry with us, what would we do?"

"What thoughts you have!" my mother said, brushing the dust from my cheeks with her leaves. "Obviously, you are an intelligent girl. You know, Daughter, Lady Sun won't become angry with us just because of a few cruel and selfish people. It's possible, though, that someday her light and warmth will gradually fade and die. Then we'll have to think about another sun or remain in the dark to freeze from the cold and die."

Now where was I in the story? Oh, yes, I was saying that the warmth had reached my pit, and I had become thirsty. A little later my sap started flowing, and my skin began to dry out and crack. A large ant came running up and began walking around on top of me.

49

When I had tumbled from the basket to the ground, my skin had split, and some of my sap had oozed out and hardened under the sunshine. The large ant thrust its pincers into the sap and pulled. Then it let go. For a while it stared at the mark made by its pincers then thrust them in again. Holding its antennae straight and clinging to the ground with its feet, it began tugging so fiercely that I thought, "Now its pincers will break off." The ant exerted its strength a while longer. Finally it plucked off a piece of the hardened syrup and happily ran away from me.

About then I heard a sound. Two people jumped down into the orchard from the top of the wall and came bounding toward me. It was Saheb Ali and Pulad, and they had come to eat the fruit. They weren't afraid of the gardener's gun like the other villagers who never set foot in the orchard. But Pulad and Saheb Ali, always in bare feet and torn and patched pants, ran freely throughout the orchard. The gardener had even shot after them several times, but Pulad and Saheb Ali had run away. At that time both were seven or eight years old.

Anyway, that day they came running, jumped over me, and went to look for my mother. A little later I saw them returning, but they were very upset. From their conversation, I could tell they were angry at the gardener.

Pulad said, "You see?" All of the fruit in the orchard has been picked, and we didn't get even one piece."

"But what could we have done?" asked Saheb Ali. "For one long month that greedy ass has been sitting at the foot of the tree with his gun in his hand. He wouldn't move!"

Pulad said, "The son of a bitch! He didn't leave even one for us. Brother, how I wanted to cram one of those juicy peaches into my mouth! . . . Do you remember how many peaches we ate last year?

"As if we weren't human," complained Saheb Ali.

50

"He picks, carries and delivers everything to the landlord, the son of a bitch, and I hope it poisons him. It's all our fault because we sat on our hands and let him plunder the village."

"You know, Saheb Ali, if he doesn't give the orchard back to the village, I'll burn all the trees."

"We're cowards if we don't burn them."

"We're not our fathers' children if we don't burn them."

The boys were extremely angry and stamped their feet so that I suddenly became afraid they would kick me. But no, they didn't. I was right in front of them when Pulad stepped on a thorn. He was bending over to take it out when his eyes fell on me, and he forgot the thorn in his foot. He picked me up from the ground. "Look, Saheb Ali!" he said.

The children happily handed me back and forth. They didn't have the heart to eat me in that condition. I was very warm. I wanted them to cool me and then eat me so I would taste better. Their dirty, calloused hands scratched my skin, but I was happy for I knew they'd eat me to the last bit with relish and after eating me, would lick their lips and fingers. And for days and weeks, they'd remember how I tasted.

"Pulad, I bet we've never seen such a large peach before."

"No, we haven't," Pulad agreed.

"Let's go over to the pool," suggested Saheb Ali. "Let's cool it and then eat it. It'll taste better."

They handled me carefully as if my body had been made of delicate glass and would fall and break with one little shake.

At the side of the pool it was shady and cool. Willows and grafted elm trees cast such a cool shade that I felt the first refreshing breeze even in my pit. They carefully put me into the water and made a fence with their four calloused little hands to prevent the water from catching me and carrying me into the pool. The water was very cold.

After they had been sitting a while, Pulad said, "Saheb Ali."

"Huh, what?"

"I'd say this peach is worth a lot," said Pulad.

"Right."

"'Right', that's not saying much," Pulad objected. "If you know, tell me how much."

Saheb Ali thought a while, then said, "I'd say it's worth a lot, too."

"For example, how much?"

Saheb Ali thought some more and said, "If we get it cold—I mean really cold!—a thousand tomans."

"You've never seen money so you think a thousand is a lot," said Pulad.

"Fine," said Saheb Ali. "You who've got so much money, you tell me how much."

"A hundred tomans."

"But a thousand is more than a hundred."

"Oh, go on," said Pulad. "I didn't make it up. I heard it from my father.

"In that case," said Saheb Ali, "maybe they're the same thing. I didn't make it up either. I heard it from my father, too."

Pulad touched me gently and said, "My hands are getting cold. I think it's time to eat it."

Saheb Ali touched me too. "Right, it's very cold."

They took me out of the water. As I came out of the water, the air felt warm. Now I wanted them to eat me quickly so I could show them I was even more delicious than they expected. I wanted to give all of the energy and warmth which I'd received from the sun and from my mother to these two peasant children.

While Pulad and Saheb Ali were deciding to eat me, I

was thinking about how often in life my circumstances had changed and how often they'd change again. I thought, "Once the particles of my body were soil, water and sunshine. My mother gradually drew nourishment from the ground and carried it up to the tips of her branches. Then she put forth buds, blossomed, and gradually I was formed. I sucked the particles of my body from my mother's body little by little and mixed them with the sunlight to form my pit, skin and flesh, and I became a ripe, juicy peach. But now Pulad and Saheb Ali are going to eat me, and a little later the particles of my body will become part of their flesh, hair and bones. Of course, they'll die someday too. Then what will the particles of my body become?"

The children decided to eat me. Saheb Ali gave me to Pulad and said, "Take a bite."

Pulad took a bite, gave me to Saheb Ali, and licked his lips. Saheb Ali took a bite and gave me back to Pulad. Just as I'd told myself I would, I tasted delicious.

Now the flesh of my body was disappearing, and my pit was thinking about a new life. A minute later no trace would remain of the peach that had been me, but my pit was planning when and how to start growing. At the same moment I would both die and come to life.

For the last time Pulad put me in his mouth, sucked my last bit of flesh, swallowed it, and took me out. I was no longer a peach. I was a living pit with a hard shell under which I concealed a new living seed. I just needed some rest and damp earth to split my shell and start growing.

When the children had licked their lips and fingers, Pulad asked, "Now what shall we do?"

"Let's go in the water."

"Aren't we going to eat the pit?" asked Pulad.

"I've got a plan for it," answered Saheb Ali. "Leave it alone."

Pulad put me down at the foot of a willow tree, made

a running start, and jumped backwards into the water, tucking his knees against his stomach and clasping his arms around them. For a moment he sank under the surface, then thrashed out his arms and legs and stood up. Mud and sediment rose from the bottom of the pool. The water reached his chin. Algae hung from his hair, ears and face.

"Pulad," said Saheb Ali, "turn the other way."

"Are you going to take off your pants?"

"Yes. I don't want my father to know we've been swimming. He'll beat me."

"We can still get home by noon," Pulad said. "We have plenty of time."

"Don't you see the sun over your head?" asked Saheb Ali.

Pulad didn't say anything else and turned the other way. When he heard Saheb Ali splash into the water, Pulad turned his face back, and they began swimming, dunking and splashing each other. Later, they reluctantly agreed that it was time to go and came out of the water. Pulad wrung out his pants legs. They picked me up from the foot of the willow and went on their way, climbing up the wall at the end of the orchard and vaulting to the other side. The village houses were far away from the landlord's orchard.

"What's your plan for the peach pit?" Pulad inquired.

"Maybe I'll come and call you toward evening, and we can go and sit on top of the hill while I tell you about my plan."

The paths in the village were deserted except for flies and the odor of dung. A huge dog sprang down from the top of the wall landing in front of us. Pulad patted the dog and turned and went into his house. The dog squeezed in after him.

The path sloped uphill so that a little higher up, it met the roof of Pulad's house which was set into the hillside. Saheb Ali made his way over this roof. His house was a little ways farther. He grasped me tightly in his fist and jumped into his courtyard. His legs sunk up to the knees into soft, wet dung that his mother had dumped there while Saheb Ali was in the orchard. At the sound of the fall, his mother stuck her head out the opening of the house and said, "Saheb Ali, hurry. Come, take some bread and water to your father."

Saheb Ali took me to the shed and in a corner, dug a hole in the dung and buried me. After that, all I knew was blackness and the odor of dung. I don't know how many hours I stayed there. I almost fainted from the acrid odor of dung. Finally I felt the dung moving away from my face. It was Saheb Ali. He picked me up and rubbed me between his palms and against his pants once or twice until I was clean. We went back the same way we'd come until we reached the roof of Pulad's house. Pulad's mother and sister were on the roof making dung cakes for fuel and talking with the neighbor's wife while she took dry dung cakes from the wall and piled them in a heap.

Saheb Ali asked Pulad's mother where he was. "Pulad took the goat to the hillside," she replied. "He's not at home."

We found Pulad on top of the hill. He had freed his black goat to graze, and he and his dog were sitting and watching for us. I suddenly realized that the color of Pulad and Saheb Ali's skin was exactly like mine. Both of them had been out in the sun enough to be burned black.

"Okay, tell me about your plan," Pulad demanded.

"Do you want to become the owner of a peach tree?" asked Saheb Ali.

"I'd be crazy if I didn't," answered Pulad.

"Then let's go."

"What shall we do with the goat?"

"We'll leave it at home."

Pulad said, "My mother said I shouldn't bring it back until sunset."

"Then we'll leave the dog with the goat."

Pulad patted the dog on the head, scratched its ears, and said, "Take care of the goat until I get back. Okay?"

The boys ran and ran until we reached the foot of the orchard wall. Saheb Ali said, "Jump up."

"You don't have to keep your plan secret any longer," Pulad burst out. "I know what it is. We're going to plant our peach pit."

"That's right," Saheb Ali said. "We're going to plant our pit behind the dirt hill dumped at the end of the orchard. In a few years, we'll be the owners of a peach tree. You know why we can't plant it any place else."

Pulad said, "A peach tree won't grow at the top of a stony hill. Trees need water. They need soft dirt."

"Cut it out—you sound like a funeral chanter," said Saheb Ali. "I'm going up to make sure the gardener hasn't returned."

The gardener still hadn't returned from town. In a secluded corner of the orchard behind a dirt hill, Pulad and Saheb Ali dug into the ground and put me under the soil, patted their hands over me, and left.

The moist, dark earth clasped me and embraced me and clung to my body. Of course, I wasn't able to grow yet. I needed some more time before I would be strong enough.

Time passed, and from the chill that found its way under the soil, I realized that winter had arrived and snow was covering the ground. The earth was frozen to within half a foot above me, but it was so warm underground that I didn't get cold and freeze. I was inactive for a time, sinking into a pleasant sweet sleep under the soil. I slept so that in spring I would wake up stronger and prepared to come out of the earth and become a tree full of fruit for Pulad and Saheb Ali—a tree full of large, juicy peaches with rose-colored cheeks like beautiful, bashful girls.

I don't remember much of my dreams throughout the

winter. I only know that once I dreamed I had become a large tree. Pulad and Saheb Ali climbed me and shook my branches, and all of the barely clad village children gathered around, tossing my peaches into the air and eating them with relish. Saliva trickled from their mouths, streaking their bare chests, stomach and navels. A child bald from ringworm repeatedly called, "Pulad, you haven't told us the name of what we're eating. After all, when I go home, I want to tell my grandmother what I've been eating. I've eaten a lot, but it's so delicious that I'm not full yet, and I'm ready to eat more. And I'm willing to bet that I won't be full even then!"

There were two little children who had nothing at all on their bodies, and patches of flies were clustered around their noses and mouths and their little penises. The children exclaimed with each large peach that they picked up and bit into. That was one of my dreams.

My last dream was about an almond flower. I was still unconscious when suddenly a soft voice rose, and at the same time, I smelled many familiar odors coming into the earth. The voice said, "Almond Flower, come forward and fan your perfume in the face of the beautiful peach. If she still doesn't wake up, stretch out your hands and place them on her face and body so that she will recognize the smell of flowers. After all, the sooner you wake her the better, for it's time to surface and sprout. All of the pits are waking up."

The perfume of the almond flower and her hands which moved over my body and face were so pleasing that I wanted to stay unconscious forever. But I didn't. I came to. I wanted to faint again but the almond flower smiled and said, "Don't resist any longer. You have a living seed inside you, and you've decided to grow and become a large tree and produce fruit. Isn't that so?"

The almond flower was like a beautiful bride who'd put on a dress of clean white snow and reddened her lips.

Of course, I'd never seen snow. I'd only heard about snow from my mother when I was a peach.

I wanted to know who'd been talking to the almond flower and who'd brought her to me. The almond flower threw her arms around my neck, kissed me and laughingly said, "What a large body you have! There's not enough room for you in my arms." After that she said, "Spring is here. It's time to surface and sprout."

Upon hearing the name Spring, I realized I was sleeping and woke up. I thought that spring had come and gone, and I still hadn't split my shell. With this thought I came wide awake in distress and confusion. I saw the dark, moist soil embracing and caressing me. My shell was soaked on the outside and sweating on the inside. Drops of water were pouring down on me from above, sliding down the sides of my body, and going under me into the earth. Several herb seeds around me were spreading their roots. One of them was growing very quickly and seemed to break out of the earth. The delicate roots moved this way and that way to suck up bits of food and water. There was another novice growing a little root, bending its head, and patiently boring a hole in the soil and inching upward. It had decided to break ground and see the sun within two days.

A new root came along under my body and tickled me with every movement as it crept forward and stretched out. The root said it belonged to the almond tree at the edge of the brook. The almond root fiercely sucked up all the moisture of the soil and bits of food and drew them in.

The water pouring down on me was from the snow melting on the ground and stopped several days later.

One day I heard a rustling sound, and a little later, an army of shifty black ants reached me and began to sting and bite me. The ants brought the warmth of the sun and the smell of the spring air into the earth. From their stings, I realized they were building a tunnel. They stung me for a while, and when they saw they couldn't dig a hole in me, they turned and burrowed in another direction. I didn't see them again until I had emerged from the earth and become a tree.

I absorbed so much water that I swelled up, and my shell broke. I sent my little roots like white filaments out of the crack in my shell. I pushed them into the soil to grow until I could depend on them to supply my food. Then I thrust out my little stalk and taught it to bend its head and face upward to pierce a hole in the dirt, find the sun, and grow tall. The tip of my stalk had a little sprout from which I could form a leaf when I emerged from the earth. Until my root became strong and was able to gather food, I ate from my stored food and fed it to my little root and my little stalk.

I had air in the soil as well, so that I wouldn't faint. The outside warmth reached into the soil again.

I was no longer a pit. I had grown inside myself, disappeared, and turned into something else. Of course, when I was a pit, I was a completely developed pit and wasn't able to grow or move any more. However, now that I was about to become a tree, I was an entirely incomplete tree and yet had plenty of space to grow and move. I thought perhaps the difference between a complete pit and an incomplete tree is that the complete pit has arrived at a dead end, and if it doesn't change, will rot, whereas the incomplete tree has an excellent future. Everything changes from second to second, and when these changes accumulate and are measured carefully, the thing is not what it was previously but is something else. For example, I myself was no longer a pit but was a seedling. I had a root and a little stalk, and I had assembled my two little yellow leaves on top of my head. I constantly grew taller. I wanted to spread my leaves in the sunshine when I came out of the ground so the sun would color them green. I developed thoughts of branches full of blossoms and juicy peaches and fallen flowers. I was an insignificant little tree; in spite of this, what a bright future lay before me! . . .

A little stone the size of a walnut barred my way and prevented me from moving farther upward. I saw that I couldn't bore a hole in it and had to circle around it to continue growing.

The taller I became, the more warmth from the sunshine I could feel and the more I turned in the direction of the sun. Now I was moving among the roots of the grass on the ground. Soon I had reached the level where some sunlight was glowing through. I realized there wasn't much crust remaining over my head. A few hours later, with a final push, I broke ground and saw the light and warmth which was waiting to greet me. I was now on the surface of the earth which was my mother's mother and is my mother and the mother of all living things.

The almond tree, white all over, sparkled in the sunshine from the other side of the dirt hill and was so happy she made me happy to the bottom of my heart. I said, "Hello."

"Hello, you beautiful thing!" replied the almond tree. "Welcome to the surface! What's going on underground?"

The herb bushes had grown tall and threw shadows, but I still had only two pale little leaves and was slowly straightening my head.

The day Pulad and Saheb Ali came to find me, I had ten or twelve green leaves and was taller than some plants, but the herb bushes were now much taller than I. I was amazed at how quickly they grew. At first I thought they would be taller than the almond tree as well in several days. Then I became aware that they didn't have strong veins and roots in the ground and told myself that the herb bushes would soon wither and die.

Pulad and Saheb Ali were happy to see me. "Now this is our tree!" they exclaimed. They brought several handfuls of water from the stream, poured them at my feet, and left. The gardener seemed to be watering sections near-by. You could hear the sound of his shovel.

Towards the end of spring I noticed that the herb bushes had stopped growing. They formed blossoms, scattered seeds, and gradually turned yellow. When summer arrived I was as tall as they were, but I still didn't have branches. I wanted to grow a little taller before producing a branch.

Pulad and Saheb Ali came to visit me often and sometimes sat for a while and talked about my future and their own plans. One day they brought a large, red, glittering snake whose head they had apparently shattered with a club. They dug into the ground a foot away from me and buried the snake.

Pulad clapped his hands and said, "I bet she'll really enjoy it!" Of course, he was referring to me.

"One snake is equal to several loads of fertilizer and dung," said Saheb Ali.

"I think we'll be eating its first fruit next year," Pulad predicted.

"I don't know," cautioned Saheb Ali. "We haven't had a tree before."

"So what," Pulad said, "I've heard that peach trees are early producers." I knew that too. My mother produced her first two peaches at age two.

I wondered how I would look when my peaches were large and ripe. I wanted to produce fruit as soon as possible to see how the peaches would suck the sap from my body. I wanted my peaches to be heavy and bend my branches so their tips would drag down to the ground.

Summer passed and autumn came. I constructed narrow veins in my body to send up whatever my roots obtained from the soil. In the middle of fall, I closed off my veins in several places, and my roots no longer sent sap upward. Then my leaves didn't receive any more food and began to turn yellow. I pinched off their stems, and the wind blew them to the ground, and I became naked.

I closed off the inner edge of each little leaf scar. I wanted to put a shoot at each of these the next spring and grow branches. I was thinking about my first fruit. I wanted to produce fruit at age two like my mother. I don't exactly remember whether I had four or five leaf scars at the top of my body from which I wanted to put forth buds and blossoms. I enjoyed thinking about my blossoms.

As the weather grew colder, I became sleepier; and by the time snow lay on the ground and the earth was frozen, I was fast asleep.

Pulad and Saheb Ali wrapped stubble and torn pieces of gunny sacks around me. After all, I still had soft, thin skin, and in the freezing winter weather, rabbits considered me delicious food. Besides, it was possible I might be frost-bitten, and then I would have to start over again the next spring.

When spring came, first all of my roots came to; then with the arrival of new sap, my stalk awoke, and my buds trembled and swelled a little. The water reaching me from the earth shook all of my limbs awake and made them active. I was forming tiny leaves inside my buds and would make them larger and flat when my buds opened. Now my little grain-like buds were growing a little larger. Only three of my buds remained. The others had been pecked off and eaten by a gluttonous little sparrow.

I opened three blossoms, but in the middle of the task, I realized I wouldn't be able to make all three into peaches. One of my first blossoms withered and fell. The second I raised into a little green peach, but later I wasn't able to provide it with food. It withered, and the wind blew it to the ground. Then I gathered all of my strength to form a unique peach which would cause whoever saw it to widen his eyes in amazement and whoever ate it to refrain from touching another piece of fruit throughout his lifetime.

Several days later I dropped the petals from my blossom and began to give food to the fruit inside the blossom case, making it grow until the case tore and my little green peach emerged.

My peach was growing near the tip of my head and bent me over a little from the day it was the size of an unripe almond. I was worried that if I grew my peach as big as I wanted, my back would have to bend and perhaps even break. But I never wanted to wither my peach and cast it aside because of the trouble it would cause. If you want to know the truth, I had decided to produce a thousand peaches the next year so it was necessary to test myself from the beginning with the first peach. The snake which the children had buried near me had now decomposed and enrichened the soil around me. Thanks to this dead snake, I became the owner of fine branches and leaves.

Pulad and Saheb Ali came to see me less often these days. I thought they were with their fathers in the fields or had gone to help with the reaping and threshing.

But one day they came to see me and drove a stick into the ground at my side and fastened me to it. I think it was that very same day that Pulad suddenly said, "Saheb Ali!"

"Huh, what?"

"I hope that son of a bitch doesn't find our tree!" Pulad blurted out.

"What if he does?" asked Saheb Ali.

Pulad didn't say anything. Saheb Ali went on, "He can't do anything. We planted the tree ourselves and brought it up; its fruit belongs to us."

Pulad thought a moment. Then he said, "The land doesn't belong to us."

"He still can't do anything," Saheb Ali retorted. "The land belongs to whoever cultivates it. This little piece of land where we planted the tree belongs to us."

Pulad found his courage and said, "Of course it belongs to us. If he does anything, I'll burn the whole orchard."

Saheb Ali struck his bare, sun-burnt chest with his fist. "May this body die if I ever allow him a moment of peace! We'll set it on fire and escape."

If Pulad and Saheb Ali hadn't given me the stick that day, I surely would have broken down at night. For a strong wind rose and beat at my branches and leaves, and in the morning I saw that several limbs of the almond tree had fallen down.

The days passed by one after another, and I grew my peach larger and larger with all of my strength and allowed the sun to put color in her cheeks and warmth to enter her flesh. My daughter clung so firmly to my body to suck my sap that sometimes I ached, but I never became angry with her. After all, now I was a mother and had a beautiful daughter.

Saheb Ali and Pulad were so beguiled by me that they almost forgot the other trees in the garden and didn't lie in wait for my mother's peaches as usual. I belonged to them and gave them the right to pick my peach when she would be completely ripe and eat her with enjoyment just as they had eaten me.

One day in early autumn, Pulad came to see me, alone and sad. It was the first time I had seen one of the boys by himself. First Pulad gave me water then sat on the grass and very slowly said to me and my peach, "My peach tree, my pretty peach, do you know what has happened? Do you have any idea why I am alone today? Of course I realize that you don't know. Saheb Ali is dead. A snake bit him . . . 'Old Woman Munjuq' attended him all night, but I don't think she did any good. Saheb Ali's father and I went and got all of the herbs she wanted from the mountains and desert, but Saheb Ali didn't get better. Poor Saheb Ali! . . . Why did you go and leave me alone?"

Pulad began to cry. Then he started to talk again. "Several days before, we had met at the top of the hill as I was returning from outside of the village at noon. We decided to go and catch a snake to fertilize your soil like we did last year. We went to the Valley of Snakes. In the Valley of Snakes there are more snakes than you could imagine. On one side of the valley is a mountain formed entirely from stone. The mountain of stone isn't solid rock. No. Imagine rather rocks of all sizes poured from the sky on top of each other into a heap. The snakes have nests in the middle of the rocks and come out to warm their bodies.

"Our land, our neighbor's land, Saheb Ali's nephew's land, and the land of several others is in the Valley of Snakes. The hissing of snakes can always be heard on this land.

"Saheb Ali and I looked at the rocks at the foot of the mountain and thrust our sticks into holes to find a fat snake for you. We were half naked. I had on only a pair of pants. My back was so hot you could have cooked an egg on it. We were hopping from rock to rock when suddenly Saheb Ali's foot slipped, and he lurched backwards and suddenly screamed, filling the valley with his pain. Saheb Ali had toppled backwards on a rock where a snake lay coiled. Saheb Ali screamed again and slid to the ground. I didn't give the snake another opportunity. I hit it at the base of the head and then the stomach and then the head again. Two mice and a sparrow were in his stomach.

"Saheb Ali was unconscious. His stick had fallen down I don't know where. The snake bite became red. If the snake had bitten his leg or arm, I would have known what to do. But in the middle of his back, what could I have done? Helpless, I put Saheb Ali on my back and carried him to the village. In the morning at his grave side, 'Old Woman Munjuq' said to my mother that if I'd brought Saheb Ali to her sooner, he wouldn't have died.

But how could I have been any faster? Peach Tree, you yourself know that Saheb Ali was heavier than I. If I owned a donkey and still had been slow, then 'Old Woman Munjuq' would have reason to say it was my fault. But what could I have done? . . ."

Pulad began to cry again. I now felt how much I loved Saheb Ali and Pulad. When I realized I wouldn't see Saheb Ali again, I almost dropped all my leaves from intense grief to become dry and budless forever.

Pulad stopped crying and continued, "I can't stay in the village any longer. Everywhere I go I see Saheb Ali's face before my eyes, and I grieve. When I go to the mountain, bring the goat to the hillside, pet the dogs, step in dung, when I catch grasshoppers and lizards with the others in the fields, when I cut hay or walk over the roof tops, Saheb Ali's face is always in front of me. I have the feeling that he's calling: Pulad! . . . Pulad! . . . Peach Tree, I can't bear hearing this call. I'm going to town to stay with my uncle and become a grocer's apprentice. I don't know what I should have done to keep Saheb Ali alive. I don't know what I should do either so that I won't suddenly die like him. I'm young. I understand very little. But I do know that I can't stay in the village. I'm going, Peach Tree. You can keep your peach for yourself."

When I saw that Pulad was going to stand up and leave, I dropped my peach in front of his feet. Pulad took the peach, smelled it, then brushed off the dirt and put his two hands around me from the bottom of my trunk to the tip of my head and left.

I grew well the next year and produced abundant branches and leaves all over my body. I had twenty or thirty blossoms and was able to raise my head higher from the hill of dirt, peek out, and see the other parts of the orchard.

One day the gardener noticed me peeking around and came to look at me. He was so happy he didn't know what to do. From the shape and color of my leaves and blossoms, he realized whose daughter I was. A fine peach tree had grown in his garden without any effort on his part. I was very disturbed to have ultimately fallen into the hands of a gardener who was the servant of a rich person and who had made the peasants his enemies for the sake of money.

I had ripened ten or fifteen peaches, but when I thought about who would get my peaches, I didn't like myself. Pulad and Saheb Ali had planted me and raised me, and only they had the right to eat my peaches. From the very day that this thought occurred to me, I began to drop my peaches.

When the gardener noticed that my peaches didn't stay with me, he thought that my location was to blame. In a very loud voice he said, "Next year I'll move you so that you can drink enough water and produce large, lovely peaches."

The next spring when I woke my roots, I saw that their neat arrangement had been disrupted. Some of the roots had dried out entirely, and some had been pulled off. Of course I still had many healthy roots. First I began to thrust my healthy roots into moist soil, and then I produced new roots and sent them out. Later I fell to thinking about budding, leaves and blossoms and greeting my mother.

I don't know how many years of my life have passed by since then. The gardener hasn't been able to eat my peaches and won't eat them in the future. He can plead with me, frighten me, or saw me down, but I won't obey him.

The Little Sugar Beet Vendor

Several years ago, I was the teacher in a village. Our school had just one room with a door and a window to the outside. It was no more than a hundred meters from the village. I had thirty-two students: fifteen in first grade, eight in second, six in third and three in fourth.

I had been sent to the school toward the end of fall. The children had been without a teacher for two or three months; they were excited to see me and raised a hubbub. School didn't really get going for four or five days. Finally I was able to gather the students from the barren hills, the carpet weaving workshop, and from wherever else they had wandered when school shut down and bring them to class.

I hadn't been in the village more than ten days when it started to snow and the ground froze. We stuck paper in the cracks in the door and window so the cold wouldn't come in.

One day the sun came out and the snow grew soft and sticky. From the room where I was giving dictation to the third and fourth grades, I could watch the first and second graders as they played. I noticed that the children had gathered around a stray dog and were pelting its head with snowballs. In the summer they went after dogs with stones and hunks of dirt, in the winter with snowballs.

A little later, my dictation was interrupted by a thin voice on the other side of the door. "Yes, I've brought sugar beets, my friends! . . . I've brought hot, sweet sugar beets! . . ."

I asked the class monitor, "Mash Kazem, who's that?"

"It must be Tarvardi, Sir . . . He sells sugar beets in the winter . . . If you want, I'll tell him to come in."

I opened the door and Tarvardi came in with his earthenware pot of sugar beets. An old cotton shawl was wrapped around his head. On one foot he was wearing a rubber boot and on the other an ordinary man's shoe. His jacket was much too big for him and reached his knees, his hands in its sleeves. The tip of his nose was red from the cold. He was no more than twelve years old.

He said hello, put the pot on the ground and asked, "Will you let me warm my hands, Sir?" The children drew him over to the stove. I offered him my chair, but he didn't sit down. He said, "No, Sir. I can sit on the floor."

The other children had come in from the snow at the sound of Tarvardi's voice, and the classroom grew disorderly. I settled them all in their places. When Tarvardi was a little warmer, he asked, "Would you like a sugar beet, Sir?"

And without waiting for my answer, he went to his sugar beets and pushed aside the dirty, colorful handkerchief covering the pot. A "Sardari" horn-handled knife was on top of the sugar beets. Tarvardi selected a sugar beet and gave it to me saying, "It would be better if you peel it yourself, Sir . . . Maybe my hands . . . After all, we're villagers . . . We haven't been to town . . . We don't know good habits."

He spoke like a wise old man. I peeled the sugar beet in the palm of my hand. The dirty skin came off, and the bright beautiful red emerged. I took a bite. It was very sweet.

From the back of the classroom, Noruz said, "Sir . . . No one's sugar beets are as sweet as Tarvardi's . . . Sir."

Mash Kazem said, "Sir, his sister cooks them and he sells them . . . His mother is sick, Sir."

I looked at Tarvardi's face. A manly, sweet smile was on his lips. He had unwrapped the cotton shawl at his neck—his hair covered his ears. He said, "Everyone has a trade or occupation, Sir . . . This is what we do."

I asked, "What's wrong with your mother, Tarvardi?"

"She can't move her legs," he answered. "The village headman says she's paralyzed. I don't really know what happened, Sir."

"Your father . . . "

He interrupted me. "He's dead."

One of the children piped up, "They called him Asgar Aqa the Smuggler, Sir."

Tarvardi continued, "He was a good horseback rider. Finally one day he was shot at the top of the mountains and died. The gendarmes shot him. They shot him from the back of his horse."

We talked a little of this and that; he sold two or three rials of sugar beets to the children and left. He didn't accept money from me but said, "This time be my guest, next time you can pay me. See, we are villagers, yet we know some manners, Sir."

As Tarvardi moved through the snow toward the village, we heard his voice calling, "Ay, sugar beets! . . . I've brought sweet, hot sugar beets, people!" Two dogs hung at his side, wagging their tails.

The children told me many things about Tarvardi. His sister's name was Sulmaz, and she was two or three years older than he. When their father was alive, they had owned a house and lived comfortably. Then they became penniless. First sister and then brother went to work for Hajji

71

Qoli Farshbaf. Almost all of the children went to Hajji Qoli Farshbaf's workshop when they weren't otherwise occupied. The quickest ones earned ten or fifteen rials a day. This Hajji Qoli had come to the village from town because town workers demanded pay in advance, receiving a minimum of forty rials a day, while the top wage in the village was thirty-five rials. Tarvardi and his sister had a dispute with Hajji Qoli and left.

Reza Qoli said, "Sir, Hajji Qoli annoyed his sister. He looked at her with dishonorable intentions, Sir."

Abol Fazl added, "Ah . . . Sir . . . Tarvardi wanted, Sir, to kill Hajji Qoli with a weaver's knife, ah . . ."

Tarvardi stopped by school once or twice every day. Sometimes when his sugar beets were gone, he came and sat in class and listened to the lesson.

One day I said to him, "Tarvardi, I heard you had a quarrel with Hajji Qoli. Can you tell me what happened?"

"It's all in the past, Sir," said Tarvardi. "It'll only give you a headache."

"I really want to hear from your own tongue what happened," I replied.

Then Tarvardi began, saying, "Forgive me, Sir. My sister and I worked for Hajji Qoli from the time we were children . . . I mean, my sister went there before I did. I worked under her direction, she got twenty rials, and I got a little less. It happened two or three years ago. My mother got sick again. She didn't work, but she wasn't bed-ridden either. Thirty or forty other children were in the workshop—are now too—and we had five or six master workmen. My sister and I went in the morning and returned at noon. My sister wore a veil in the workshop but didn't cover her face . . . There were the master workmen who were like fathers to us and the other children, and Hajji Qoli was the owner.

Sir, near the end of our time in the workshop, Hajji Qoli would shamelessly come and stand over the two of us.

He would stare at my sister and, sometimes placing his hand on her head or my head, would laugh for no apparent reason and pass by. I didn't think anything of it as he was our employer, and I thought he was just being kind. Some time passed. One Thursday when we were getting our weekly wages, he gave an extra ten rials to my sister and said, "Your mother is sick, spend this on her."

"Then he laughed into my sister's face in a way I disliked. My sister seemed frightened; she didn't say anything. And the two of us, Sir, went back to our mother. When she heard that Hajji Qoli had given my sister some extra money, she thought for a moment and said, "After this, don't accept extra money."

"From the next day on, I saw that the master workmen and older children whispered among themselves and spoke into each other's ears as if they didn't want my sister and me to hear.

"Sir, the next Thursday we went to get our wages after everyone else. Hajji had told us to come and see him when he was alone. Hajji, Sir, gave me fifteen extra rials and said, 'Tomorrow I'm coming to your house. I have something to say to your mother.'

"Then he laughed into my sister's face in a way I disliked. My sister grew pale and lowered her head.

"Forgive me, Sir. You told me to tell it all—I threw Hajji's fifteen rials at him and said, 'Hajji Aqa, we don't need extra money. My mother doesn't like it.'

"Hajji laughed again and said, 'Don't be a fool, my boy. It's not for you or your mother to like or dislike it . . . '

Then he picked up the fifteen rials and was about to thrust them into my sister's hand when she drew back and ran out. I began crying in anger. There was a weaver's knife on the table. I grabbed it and threw it. The knife cut Hajji's face, and the wound started to bleed. Hajji shouted for help. I ran out, and I don't know what happened after that. I went home. My sister was there crouched at my mother's side crying.

That night, Sir, the village headman came. Hajji Qoli had complained about me and had said, 'I want to become a part of their family; otherwise, I'll turn the boy over to the gendarmes and they'll fix him.' The village headman went on, 'Hajji sent me to ask for the hand of your daughter. Yes or no?'

"Hajji Qoli's wife and children are in town, Sir. He has concubines in four other villages. Excuse me, Sir. He's just like a huge pig—fat and squat with a short black and white beard and artificial teeth, some of them gold, and a long string of worry beads in his hand. God preserve you from ever being like him—a huge pig, old and decrepit.

"My mother said to the village headman, 'Even if I had a hundred daughters, I wouldn't give one of them to that hyena. We've suffered enough. Headman, you yourself know that kind of person isn't really interested in having family connections with us villagers . . . '

"The village headman, Sir, said, 'Yes, you're right. Hajji Qoli wants a concubine. But if you don't consent, he'll kick the children out of his workshop; then there's the problem of the gendarmes and so on . . . You should take this into account, too!'

"My sister, crouched behind my mother, said between her sobs, 'I'm not going to the workshop any more . . . He'll kill me . . . I'm afraid of him . . .

"In the morning my sister didn't go to work. I went alone. Hajji Qoli was standing at the door, fingering his worry beads. I was afraid, Sir; I didn't go any closer. Hajji Qoli, who had bound the wound on his face with cloth, said, 'Come on inside, boy; I'm not going to hurt you.'

"I very fearfully went closer to him and was just about to go through the door when he grabbed my wrist, threw me into the workshop courtyard and fell upon me, hitting and kicking. Finally I struggled loose and ran to pick up the weaver's knife from the table. He had beat on me so much that my body was aching and bruised. I screamed, 'You dirty pimp, now I'll show you who you're dealing with . . . They call me Son of Asgar Aqa the Smuggler . . . '"

Tarvardi took a fresh breath and went on again, "Sir, I was about to kill him right then and there. The workers gathered around and carried me home by force. I was crying in anger and throwing myself on the ground and swearing. Blood poured from the spot on my face where Hajji had hit me . . . At last I grew quiet.

"We had a goat. My sister and I had bought it for two hundred rials. We sold it and got through the next month or two on the bit of money we had saved. Finally, my sister went to work for the woman who bakes bread, and I did whatever work was available . . ."

I said, "Tarvardi, why doesn't your sister get married?"

"The son of the bread baking woman is her fiancé," he replied. "My sister and I are preparing a dowry so they can get married."

This summer I visited the same village again. I saw Tarvardi out on the barren hillsides with forty or fifty goats and sheep. I asked him, "Tarvardi, did your sister's dowry turn out all right?"

He said, "Yes. She got married, too . . . Now I'm saving money for my own marriage. After all, since my sister moved to her husband's house, my mother has been without help. She needs someone to give her a hand and talk to her . . . But I'm being impolite with all this chatter . . . Forgive me, Sir."

The Bald Pigeon Keeper

A few words:

Children, the future is in your hands and its good and evil belong to you. Whether you want to or not, you are growing up as time passes. You come after your fathers and elders and will take their places and inherit everything. You will be master of society. Poverty, oppression, power, justice, joy and sorrow, loneliness, punishment, work and idleness, prison and freedom, sickness and hunger and need, and a hundred strengths and weaknesses of society will belong to you.

We know that in order to cure an illness, one must first find the cause of that illness. For example, doctors, in order to treat their patients, first isolate the bacteria causing the disease and then give the appropriate medicine to their patients. The same thing must be done to eliminate the ills of society. We know that disease is never found in a healthy body. Signs of disease must not exist in a healthy society either. Poverty, oppression, lies, stealing, and war are illnesses seen only in an unhealthy society. In order to cure all of these illnesses, their causes must be found. Always ask yourselves: Why has my classmate and friend been sent to work in a carpet weaving workshop? Why do some people steal? Why are war and bloodshed everywhere? What do we become after death? What were we before life? What will finally happen to the world? When will war, poverty and hunger come to an end?

You must ask a thousand other questions to understand society and its problems. Remember that society isn't contained within the four walls of your homes. Society includes all places where our fellow countrymen live—isolated villages with dung-filled alleys and dark huts full of flies as well as towns and cities with clean avenues and chic bright mansions of rich city dwellers. Society includes children of peasants, carpet weavers, workers and beggars as well as children whose everyday food is chicken and rice, turkey, bananas and oranges. All of this is the society you will inherit from your fathers. But you must not pass this inheritance untouched on to your own children. You must reduce its ills and eliminate problems, increase its strong points, and find medicine for its diseases and eventually eradicate them. Society isn't a trust fund to be left just as is.

There are several ways to become familiar with society and find answers to its questions. One way is to visit villages and towns and associate with different kinds of people. Another way is to read books. Of course not all books. Some people say, "Every book is worth reading once." Such talk is nonsense. There are so many good books in the world we don't live long enough to read even a fourth of them. We must choose the books which give the right answers to our various questions; describe objects, events and phenomena; acquaint us with our own society and with other nations; and show us the troubles of society. Books which merely entertain us and mislead us are good only for tearing up and burning.

Children like to read fairy tales and stories. Worthwhile stories can teach you about people, society, and life and explain causes. Reading stories need not be solely for entertainment. I want perceptive children to learn from my stories as well as be entertained by them.

Behrangi

Long ago, a young man lived with his old mother. Because he was completely bald from a scalp disease, the young man was called Kachal [Bald One]. Their home had a small yard with a mulberry tree under which a bald black goat fed, chewed its cud, shook its beard, pawed the ground with its hoofs and baaed. Their room faced Mecca and had a small window, a hole for an oven in the middle, a platform across from the door and an opening in the roof for smoke, light, air and so on. Instead of glass they had fastened straw paper over the window. The walls were mud and straw with nooks and crannies dug in all around.

Every morning Kachal would go out to the barren hillsides, cut thistles and grass, put them in a bundle and carry the bundle home. He would give some of the grass to the goat and store the rest on the roof so that in winter he could sell it or feed it to his goat. Every afternoon he would fly pigeons. He was a good pigeon trainer and had ten or fifteen pigeons. He whistled well too. From morning to night the old woman would sit at her spinning wheel and spin yarn. In this way, the mother and son earned their living.

The king's beautiful palace looked down on their hut. The king's daughter had fallen in love with Kachal and whenever Kachal flew his pigeons from the roof, she would come out on the balcony with her maids and slaves to watch him training pigeons and listen to his whistling.

Sometimes she would speak to Kachal with her eyes and with gestures. But Kachal didn't pay any attention. He behaved as if he weren't aware of the girl. Actually, Kachal was also deeply in love with the king's daughter, but he didn't want her to know it. He realized the king would never give his daughter to a bald peasant who had only a goat, ten or fifteen pigeons and an old mother to his name. And even if he would, the king's daughter couldn't move into their smoke-filled hut and stay there.

No matter what the king's daughter did, she wasn't able to get Kachal to talk with her. One day she even punched holes in a sheep's heart, to symbolize how Kachal's love had pierced her heart, and hung it in front of her window, but Kachal still ignored her. He flew his pigeons at the edge of the pile of thistles, whistled, and listened to the sound of his mother's spinning wheel.

Finally, the king's daughter became ill. She didn't come out to the balcony anymore and didn't watch Kachal from the window. The king gathered all the doctors to see his daughter, but none could make her well.

All storytellers at such a point say, "The king's daughter didn't reveal her heart's secret to anyone," whether from fear or shyness or in modesty, but I say that the king's daughter finally told her heart's secret to her father. When the king heard that his daughter was in love with the bald pigeon trainer, he became angry and shouted, "If I hear the name of that scum on your tongue again, I'll send you packing! Are there so few men that you have to fall in love with that scum? I'm going to marry you off to the vazir's son. And that's final."

The girl didn't say anything. The king went and sat on his throne, and summoned the vazir before him. "Vazir," he ordered, "you must cut off the heads of the bald man's pigeons this very day and prohibit him from going up on the roof anymore."

The vazir sent several of his own strong men to

Kachal's house. Kachal, completely unaware of what was going on, was feeding his pigeons when the king's men burst into his hovel. In the wink of an eye, they cut off the pigeons' heads and beat up Kachal, battering and bruising his entire body. They broke one foot of the old woman's spinning wheel as well, and tore the paper covering from the window before they left.

Kachal didn't move for a week. He lay moaning in his hut. The old woman put myrrh on his wounds and cursed. After a week had passed, Kachal came out and sat under the mulberry tree to get some fresh air and cheer himself up. He was thinking about where to bury his pigeons when he heard a voice over his head. He looked up and saw that two pigeons, perched on the mulberry tree, were talking to each other.

One of the pigeons said, "Sister dear, do you know who this boy is?"

"No, Sister dear."

"This is the boy," the first pigeon explained, "for the love of whom the king's daughter became sick and is bedridden. The king gave an order to his vazir, and the vazir sent his servants to kill the boy's pigeons. They beat him and put him out of commission until today. Now he's thinking about where to bury his pigeons."

"Why is he going to bury them?" asked the second pigeon.

"What else can he do?"

"When we fly off," said the second pigeon, "four leaves will fall from our feet. If he feeds them to his goat and rubs the goat's milk on the heads and necks of his pigeons, they'll come alive and will perform as no pigeon ever has before . . . "

"I hope he can hear our conversation! . . . " the first pigeon said.

The pigeons flew up into the air; four leaves were torn off beneath their feet. Kachal caught them in midair

81

and immediately fed them to the goat. Her udders soon filled with milk. Kachal brought a bowl, milked the goat, and rubbed some milk on the heads and necks of the pigeons. The pigeons came alive, flapped their wings, and lifted into the air to encircle Kachal.

The old woman came out at the sound of the pigeons flapping their wings. Kachal told her what had happened. "My dear son, give up training pigeons," she pleaded. "The next time you go up on the roof, the king will kill you."

"Mother, my pigeons aren't like any pigeons you've ever seen before. Watch . . . " Then Kachal said to his pigeons, "My lovely pigeons, do something to make me happy and satisfy my mother." The pigeons, gathering in a circle, began to whisper and suddenly flew up and away into the air. Kachal and his mother waited. Some time passed. There was no sign of the pigeons. "So this is the loyalty of your lovely pigeons! . . . " the old woman said.

She hadn't even finished her sentence when the pigeons appeared in the sky. They brought with them a felt shepherd's hat which they gave to Kachal. The old woman said, "What a valuable gift they've brought for you. Now let's see if it fits."

Kachal put the felt hat on his head. "It looks good on me, Mother, doesn't it?"

"Son, where are you?" asked the old woman in amazement, as she looked around for her missing son.

"Mother, I'm right here."

"Let me see the hat," said the old woman.

Kachal took off the hat and gave it to his mother. The old woman put it on her head. "Mother, where are you?" shouted Kachal.

The old woman didn't answer. Kachal looked around in astonishment. Suddenly he heard the sound of his mother's spinning wheel. He ran inside and saw that the spinning wheel was turning all by itself and spinning yarn. Then he realized the hat's value. "Mother, don't tease me anymore," he said. "Give me the hat and I'll go and get some food. I'm dying of weakness and hunger."

"Swear you won't touch forbidden property, and I'll give you the hat," said the old woman.

"I swear that I won't touch things that are forbidden to me."

The old woman gave the hat to Kachal, and he put it on and went outside. Hajji Ali the weaver lived several districts over. He had some factories and hundreds of workers, servants and maids. Kachal walked along saying to himself, "Okay, Kachal, figure it out. Is Hajji Ali's property legitimate for you or not? Where has Hajji Ali gotten his money? From his factories? Does he himself work? No. He doesn't dirty his hands with labor. He merely takes the profit from the factories and enjoys himself. So who works and makes a profit, Kachal? Set your brain to work and come up with the right answer. Tell me, if the people don't work, what will happen to the factories? They'll close down, won't they? Then will the factories still make a profit? Of course not. "Well then," he muttered to himself, "the conclusion we can reach from these questions and answers is that the workers work, but Hajji Ali gets all the profit and gives them only a little. Since Hajji Ali's wealth doesn't belong to him, it's legitimate for me."

With an easy mind, Kachal entered Hajji Ali the weaver's house. Several servants and maids were going in and out of the door to Hajji Ali's outer courtyard. No one noticed Kachal. Hajji Ali and several of his wives were sitting on a platform at the edge of a pool in the inner courtyard. They were having their five o'clock tea with biscuits, honey and cream. Kachal's mouth watered. He went forward and took a large piece. Hajji Ali was looking at the honey and cream when he saw half of it disappear. He began chanting prayers and Bismillah and saying his beads. Kachal took Hajji Ali's tea from in front of him and gulped it down. This time the women and Hajji Ali screamed in terror, left everything, and ran inside. Kachal ate all of the honey and cream, drank several cups of tea, and went inside to walk around. Kachal was astounded by all of the expensive things in the house—gold and silver candle sticks, gold inlaid screens, many carpets and rugs, silver and crystal dishes, and many other things. He took everything that would fit into his pocket.

Kachal found the key to Hajji's safe. At night, when everyone was asleep, he opened the safe, took as much of Hajji's money as he could carry, and left. He robbed the homes of several other wealthy people so it was after midnight when he turned homeward. He kept a little money for himself and his mother and gave the rest to the poor families along his way.

He would knock at the door of a house. When the head of the house came to the door, Kachal would say, "Take this bit of gold and two thousand tomans, and spend it on your children. This is your share. Don't tell anyone." Before the head of the house could see who was at the door and where the voice was coming from, a fistfull of gold and a large amount of money would be poured at his feet.

Kachal got home very late. The old woman hadn't gone to sleep. She was still sitting at her spinning wheel, worrying about Kachal. Sleep filled her eyes. The pigeons had tucked their heads under their wings and were sleeping here and there in the hut. Kachal soundlessly entered the hut and sat at his mother's side. Suddenly he took the hat from his head. The old woman was very happy to see her son. "Where have you been at this time of night, Son?"

"At the house of Hajji Ali the weaver. I was taking the people's property from him."

The old woman brought groat soup for him. "I've eaten so much honey and cream that even if I don't touch food for a week, I still won't be hungry," said Kachal.

The old woman ate dinner by herself, drank some goat's milk, and then they both went to bed.

Before he went to sleep, Kachal poured the leftover groats out for the pigeons. Early the next day he put the hat on his head, went to the roof, and began flying pigeons and whistling. He held a long stick with a rag tied to its end in his hand.

The king's daughter was lying ill in bed, her eyes glued to the roof. Suddenly she saw that Kachal's pigeons were flying about, and she heard him whistling. But there was no sign of Kachal! Only the pigeon training stick could be seen moving to and fro in the air and making the pigeons perform.

The vazir's servants told the vazir, and he informed the king that Kachal had started up his mischief again, and perhaps the princess would get worse. Once more, the king sent the vazir to kill the pigeons.

The king's daughter was worried about Kachal and sent her trusted slave to the old woman to tell her that the king's daughter was in love with Kachal and that she should think of something to do.

Meanwhile Hajji Ali and others angrily poured into the prince's palace. "We've been ruined, our lives have been tossed to the winds. What kind of a king are you, anyway? Send your army after the thieves to get our property back . . . "

Let's leave all this for now, while I tell you what was going on at Kachal's house. Kachal, hat on his head, was flying pigeons on the roof; the old woman, wearing her old veil, was washing wool under the roof; and the goat was wandering around the yard, going after mulberry leaves that the wind had blown off the tree.

The old woman suddenly raised her head and saw that the goat was looking into her face. She looked back into the goat's eyes. The goat seemed to say, "Kachal and the pigeons are in danger. Bring me some mulberry leaves to eat and I'll tell you what to do."

The old woman didn't hesitate. She got up and knocked some leaves to the ground with a stick. The goat ate and ate and her stomach swelled. Then she stared into the old woman's face and seemed to say, "Thank you. Now go inside. I'll climb up to the roof and help Kachal and the pigeons."

The old woman didn't say anything and went inside. The goat went up the outside stairs, reached the pile of thistles, and began to eat again.

Nothing happened until several of the vazir's servants rushed into the yard. The pigeon training stick moved this way and that in the air, hit whoever tried to set foot on the roof, and threw him to the ground. Finally all the servants returned to the vazir.

The princess saw everything from the window and felt a little better. The scene cheered her up.

The king, Hajji Ali the factory owner, and the other wealthy people were sitting and wondering what skillful thief had burglarized all their houses in one night and had taken so much property and wealth. At this point the vazir entered. "King," he said, "something strange has happened. Kachal wasn't there himself but his pigeon training stick was flying pigeons on the roof and didn't allow anyone to get near the pigeons."

"Get Kachal and bring him to me," ordered the king.

"Kachal's nowhere to be found in the hut," objected the vazir. "His mother's alone. She doesn't know where Kachal is."

"King, this Kachal has a hand in everything that's happened," said Hajji Ali the factory owner. "All signs point to Kachal as the thief who robbed us." Then he told the story of the vanishing honey, cream and tea.

One of the other rich people said, "My wife's

necklace rose from her neck, turned to vapor, and vanished . . . in front of my very own eyes!"

"I too saw my gold-framed mirror rise into the air from the cabinet and set out," said someone else. "Before I could move, the mirror wasn't there any more. Hajji Ali is right. All of this is Kachal's doing."

The king became angry and ordered the army to prepare to seize Kachal's house and bring him out dead or alive.

At this very moment the king's daughter was sitting and talking with her trusted slave who had just returned from the old woman. "My lady, Kachal's mother told me that he's alive and very well too. Tonight she'll send him to talk with you."

"Kachal's coming to see me?" asked the king's daughter with surprise. "But how can he pass through the army and guards? I wish he could come! . . . "

"My lady," the slave said, "bald people know a thousand and one tricks. We'll wait for him tonight. He'll come for sure."

At this moment they looked out the window and saw that the army had surrounded Kachal's house like gem prongs on a ring. The king's daughter said, "Even if he has a thousand lives, he can't escape. My poor Kachal! . . . "

The pigeons were now perched on the roof eating grain. The pigeon training stick was standing upright. The goat was continuously eating thistles and dropping turds hard enough to break a head.

The army was standing at attention. "Ahoy, Kachal," shouted the army commander, "even if you have a thousand lives, not one can escape. Think about it . . . Surrender immediately. If you don't, the largest part of you left will be your ears.

The old woman trembled with fear in the hut and stopped spinning. She looked out of the hole in the ceiling but didn't see anything.

"My pretty pigeons," Kachal said, "don't you see what the goat's doing? She's making turds for you. Do something to make me happy and satisfy my mother . . ." The pigeons gathered in a circle, whispered among themselves, then flew into the air and disappeared.

The commander of the army shouted again, "Ahoy, Kachal, this is the last time I'm going to tell you. I order you to stop your tricks and mischief-making. You can't take us on. You'll be captured in the end, and regret won't help you then. Wherever you are, come out and surrender! . . . "

"Your Excellency, Commander of the Army, excuse me for keeping you waiting. I was tightening the string that holds up my pants. Otherwise I would have presented myself to you. Light up a cigarette and I'll be right there."

The commander of the army was happy that there wouldn't be any problem capturing Kachal. He lit a cigarette and called, "What a trick! . . . What stinky hole is your voice coming from?"

"From your father's grave and your mother's! . . . "

The commander of the army got angry and shrieked, "Shut up! . . . Do you think I'm someone you can fool around with?"

At this moment hundreds of pigeons appeared from all directions. Kachal's pigeons were in the midst of them. The goat gobbled thistles and dropped turds.

Kachal picked up a turd and said, "Your Excellency, Commander of the Army, watch. See where I am."

And he threw the turd at the commander of the army. The commander of the army had lifted his head and, with a cigarette in the corner of his mouth, was looking up into the air when the turd hit him between the eyebrows. He shrieked. The army rushed forward. But the pigeons didn't give them a chance. They dropped turds on the army. They took the turds in their beaks, flew up high into

the air, and released them over the army, breaking open
the heads of many of the soldiers. At night the army
retreated. Kachal took the goat and pigeons and came
down. The other pigeons left again.

With the money that Kachal had given her, the old
woman cooked a remarkable supper. It wasn't the usual
pretense of a meal: a piece of dry bread with a little groat
soup or just plain bread with water sprinkled on it. There
was wheat for the pigeons, and the goat ate alfalfa and
barley.

After supper the old woman said to Kachal, "Now
put on the hat, and go see the king's daughter. I promised I
would send you to her."

"But Mother, there's a big difference between us and
the king's daughter."

"Go and see what she has to say," said the old
woman.

Kachal put on the hat and left. He passed through the
guards and soldiers and entered the room of the king's
daughter who was eating dinner with her trusted slave. The
princess was feeling better and was saying to her slave, "If
Kachal knew how much I love him he wouldn't delay a
minute. But I'm afraid the guards will catch him and kill
him. I'm worried."

"Yes, my lady, I'm afraid too," replied the slave.
"Tonight the king ordered that the guards be doubled in
number, and he named the vazir's son commander."

Kachal went over and sat at the side of the king's
daughter and began eating. Dinner was chicken and rice
with several kinds of souffles, soups, jams and so on. The
princess and her slave suddenly saw that one side of the
tray was quickly becoming empty and a chicken leg had
been torn off and had disappeared.

"My lady, think what you like," said the slave. "I'm
sure Kachal is in the room. This is his doing. Didn't I tell
you that bald people have a thousand and one tricks! . . . "

The king's daughter brightened. "My dear Kachal, if you're here, show yourself. I miss you very much."

Kachal didn't say anything. "Maybe he's not coming out because of me," suggested the slave. "I'll go and watch out for the guards . . . "

When the slave had gone, Kachal took off his hat. At once the king's daughter saw Kachal sitting at her side. "Kachal," she said happily, "don't you know I'm deeply in love with you? Marry me! Rescue me, for the king wants to marry me off the to vazir's son."

"You're a princess, how could you endure living in our smoky hut?"

"If I were with you, I could stand anything."

"My mother and I barely make a living for ourselves; how could we afford to feed you? Besides, you're a princess and don't know how to work."

"I'll learn how to do something."

"What?"

"Whatever you say," answered the king's daughter.

"Then it's settled. I'll tell my mother to teach you how to spin. Wait for a few days. I'll come and tell you when we'll escape from here."

Let Kachal and the girl continue in tender conversation while I tell you about the vazir's son who was commander of the army and in love with the King's daughter. When Kachal had come to see the king's daughter, he saw the vazir's son slumped in his chair, sleeping. On impulse, Kachal decided to take his sword and spear. When the vazir's son woke up and didn't see his weapons, he realized that Kachal had managed to get in. Immediately, he sent all of the guards to the room of the king's daughter. A guard saw the princess's slave outside the door. He forced her aside, opened the door, and saw Kachal and the King's daughter in earnest conversation. He quickly slammed the door and shouted, "Kachal's here. Come quickly! Kachal's here."

The vazir's son and the others came running. The King was awakened by the commotion, got up on his throne, and ordered that Kachal be brought before him, dead or alive.

The commander and some of the other guards entered the girl's room. The King's daughter was lying on her bed reading a story. There was no sign of Kachal. The vazir's son asked her, "Princess, where's Kachal? A guard saw him here just a minute ago."

The girl replied sharply, "My father is completely indifferent to my honor. He gives permission to you to enter the room of his sick daughter at night, and then you are rude enough to say such things. Get out of here at once!"

The vazir's son persisted politely and respectfully, "Princess, the King himself commanded that we search every nook and cranny. I'm under orders and am not to blame." Then they searched the room. They didn't find anything except the sword and spear of the vazir's son which Kachal had brought and hidden under the bed. "Princess, these belong to me. Kachal took them from me. If he's not here, then what are these doing here? I'll report this to the King."

At this very moment, Kachal was standing at the side of the King's daughter and saying into her ear, "Don't be afraid. Don't change your expression. I'll come after you shortly."

Then he passed by the guards to the door. Three or four of the guards were standing right at the threshold, and he couldn't get by. He was about to shove his way through and escape when suddenly he stumbled against something, and his hat fell off.

No matter how much Kachal pleaded for them to give back his hat since it was bad to go before the King with a bare head, the vazir's son didn't listen.

The king was sitting angrily on his throne and

91

waiting. When Kachal reached his throne, he shouted, "Bastard, I can forgive all of your other mistakes—you plunder people's homes, you have vanquished my army— but how dare you enter my daughter's room? I'm going to order my vazir to come immediately and pour molten lead down your throat."

"King, whatever you command is all right with me. But first tell them to untie my hands and give me my hat. It's bad manners to be in the presence of the King with my head uncovered and my hands not folded over my chest."

The King ordered that his hands be unbound and his hat returned to him. The vazir's son didn't want to return the hat but he didn't dare disobey the King. Kachal put on the hat and became invisible. The King jumped up. "Boy," he shouted, "where did you go? Why are you hiding?"

"Your Majesty, he didn't go anywhere," broke in the vazir's son fearfully. "He's hiding under his hat; order the doors to be locked or he'll escape."

Before he could get going and sneak out, Kachal found himself caught in a trap. The guard surrounded the King's chambers so securely that not even a mouse would be able to find an escape hole.

When the King saw that he couldn't capture Kachal, he called for an executioner. "Executioner, cut off the head of the vazir's bastard! . . ." ordered the King. The vazir's son fell to his hands and knees and begged for mercy. "You bastard," the King retorted, "since you knew what kind of a hat it is, why didn't you tell me? . . . Executioner, show no mercy. Cut off his head!" And so it happened that the vazir's son was killed in the middle of the night.

Now let's get back to the King's daughter. When she saw that Kachal was trapped and the vazir's son had been killed, she said to her slave, "Don't you realize that if the vazir comes, he'll get us mixed up in this too? So why should we sit here and do nothing? Get up—let's go see

Kachal's mother. Perhaps we'll think of something to do. I'm about to lose my poor Kachal!"

The busy guards didn't notice their departure. Kachal's mother was sitting alone washing wool. The goat and the pigeons were sleeping. The King's daughter told the old woman how Kachal had been trapped and urged her to do something.

The old woman thought a moment, then went to wake the goat and pigeons. "Aha, my smart, bushy bearded goat, aha my pretty, bald pigeons, my son has been trapped at the King's house. Do something to make my Kachal happy and satisfy me. This is the King's daughter who wants to be my daughter-in-law. Free her from grief! . . . "

The goat asked for something to eat. The old woman and the girls brought it thistles and mulberry leaves, and it began to eat and drop turds. The pigeons went and found their friends. The old woman made a fire and put the bread sheet over it to roast wheat for the pigeons.

The pigeons ate the wheat, picked up the turds, flew up into the air, and dropped them on the heads of the army and guards. They kept at it throughout the dark night.

By now news had reached the vazir. He went to the King and said, "King, if this continues for another hour or two, the pigeons will bring the door and walls crashing down on top of us. Perhaps we should free Kachal and then sit down and think up a new approach."

The King agreed and ordered the doors to be opened. "Ahoy, Kachal," he shouted, "get your stinking self out of here. Someday I'll get even with you."

Several silent minutes passed. Then Kachal called from the courtyard, "Your Majesty, I'd like to take advantage of this opportunity to inform you that nowhere are suitors treated like this . . . ."

"Fool, you're too lowly to be my daughter's suitor!"

"King, give me your daughter's hand, and I'll tell the pigeons to quiet down. Your daughter and I are in love."

"I don't need such a shameless daughter. I'm going to kick her out immediately . . . ."

The King sent several servants after his daughter to throw her out of the house. The servants returned, saying, "King, your daughter has already left on her own."

Kachal didn't say anything else, but gestured to the pigeons and went home. His mother had given hot milk to the King's daughter and her slave.

* * *

Kachal, with the bit of gold and jewelry that the king's daughter had brought and the money that his mother, the king's daughter, and he himself earned, set up a good life for the three of them. But he still cut thistles, trained pigeons, and tied his goat up under the mulberry tree. His mother and wife washed the wool in the house. And so they supported themselves.

They freed the slave and she married. She also set up a life of her own.

Hajji Ali the factory owner and the others still came to see the King and complain about Kachal since he burglarized their homes from time to time. Of course, he never took anything for himself.

The King and vazir sat down every day to make plans and think out strategy against Kachal. The king made the vazir's younger son commander of the guards and bribed the vazir so he wouldn't say anything about the murder of his older son . . .

* * *

All storytellers say "Our story has come to an end." But I'm sure our story hasn't ended. Someday, of course, we'll continue the tale . . .

Biographical-Historical Essay
by Thomas Ricks

"Samad Behrangi and Contemporary Iran: The Artist in Revolutionary Struggle"

Each one of us lives in a home. In our homes, we respect and love our father. We also have a larger home. This large home is our country, Iran. We are like one family in this large home. The king is like the father of this family. We are like his children. The king loves all of us. We love our loving king of kings like our own father. We respect our king of kings.[1]

The First Grade Persian reader's explanation of the king's relations with the people of Iran seems innocent, feasible, and realistic. The present king's "paternal and loving" posture towards the people is an image frequently projected not only in First Grade readers but also in all phases of Iranian public life. It is the major image projected to Europe and the United States. In the words of the monarch himself in the introduction to *The White Revolution*:

Today, [1967] more than ever before, a close spiritual union exist between my nation and myself. This has been brought about not only by my resolve to dedicate my existence to the welfare and progress of the people ... but by the intrinsic respect and prestige that the institution of the monarchy and the person of the Shah have traditionally held in Iran. [2]

The purpose of this essay will therefore be to examine the "paternal" and historical ties of the Iranian people to the king and regime as well as to test the validity of the monarch's claims of "intrinsic respect and prestige" of Iranian Kingship through an examination of Samad Behrangi and Iran's writers and artists both past and present.

A closer examination of Iran's historical developments over the last one hundred and twenty years reveals an agrarian society bottom-heavy with village peasants, pastoral tribesmen, and urban workers in conflict with the urban ruling families under the leadership of the king. The outstanding events in the historical development of contemporary Iran have been 1) the Constitutional Movement (1905-1911), 2) the Nationalization of Oil and the Mossadeq Period (1941-1953), and 3) the "June Days" of 1963 to the present. In each period the revolutionary (such as, the workers' movements) and reformist (such as, the National Front) positions were present with the latter dominating the political leadership of the people in the struggle against the regime until 1963; as a result of the discrediting of the reformist leadership (particularly, the Tudeh Party and the National Front), the revolutionary position began to dominate instead. In each period, also, the writer as protagonist and advocate for the various nationalities and classes within Iran generally fell either into the revolutionary or reformist groups. The revolutionary writers more than the reformists struggled to pioneer the changes in contemporary Persian literature and in the role of the writers and artists in contemporary Iran. M. Azarm's distinctions which were made in an address to the Technical College at the University of Tehran, between "poetry of resistance," or *sh'ir-i moghavamat* and "poetry of submission," or *sh'ir-i taslim*, indicates the difference

96

between the poetry of the people, revolution, and resistance to the regime and the poetry of the palace, reaction, and praise of the current regime respectively. Finally, the literary importance of today's writers continues to be based on an ability to describe the conditions of society and the interests of the people, making clear the contradictions in the society while exposing the reactionary regime and mobilizing the people towards struggle.

One such writer, Samad Behrangi, understood his role as artist and writer within contemporary Iran. He wrote a number of important children's stories, translations of Azarbayjani folktales, and essays concerning the aspirations of the Iranian people and the social and economic contradictions within and outside of Iranian society. Moreover, he wrote about the village and urban poor not as children "loving and respecting" the king whose position in Iran was one of "intrinsic respect and prestige"; rather as a people struggling to alter the increased repression of the "White Revolution" and the growing military and economic interests of the United States and Europe. It is now clear that Behrangi's unexpected and untimely death in 1968 arose out of his role in the movement both as a teacher and a writer. Since his death, the role of artists and writers has remained the same although the conditions of maintaining that role have worsened considerably.

By 1970, the emergence of many movements seeking change, including the Iranian People's Combatants Organization, or IPCO (*mujahidin-i khalq-i Iran*), the Organization of the Iranian People's Guerrilla Fighters, or OIPGF (*sazman-i cherik'ha-yi fida'i khalq-i Iran*), and other groups, indicated the continuing need for and expression of revolutionary strategy present since 1963. While Samad Behrangi's thoughts and writings are central to this essay, an historical review is in order for perspective in any discussion of the writer in contemporary Iran.

I.

Iran's history over the last 200 years is a history of constant and continual conflict between the rural-urban lower classes-intellectuals and the king-ruling families-European coalition. From the 18th century onward, the escalation of economic, military, and political interests of Russia and Britain in the "welfare" of Iran accelerated the autocratic rule of the kings (the 19th-Century Qajars particularly), frustrated the commercial and political interests of the provincial ruling families, and increased the exploitation of the villagers and urban workers.

During the 1870's, in the midst of British-Russian concessionary haggling for Iran's lands and revenues, Nasir ed-Din Shah traveled twice to Europe on the income of the foreign loans and investments. The greater dependency of Qajar kings and the ruling families on the interests and capital of Europe and the inability of Iranian commercial classes to compete with European products and production resulted in the Tobacco Regie of 1890-1892 and the eventual assassination of Nasir ed-Din Shah in 1896; the first event being the successful confrontation of the provincial ruling families against the monarchy and Britain and, the second, the opposition of the intellectuals, or *rushanfikran.*

On the eve of the Constitutional Movement in 1905, Iranian writers were already assuming an important role in this first of many attempts to curtail the expansion of monarchical and foreign economic and political domination. The uneasy alliance of provincial ruling families, progressive merchants and religious, and reform-minded urban classes brought about the Constitution and limitations on monarchical powers of the Qajar kings. Instrumental in the proceedings in Tabriz and Tehran during the 1905-1911 period was the emerging group of revolutionary writers and *rushanfikran.*

The intellectuals, or *rushanfikran* arose principally out of the events of the 1850's. With a new level of political consciousness, there also arose new methods of communicating the political awareness, principally through journalism and essay-writing (principally published in the journals *Qanun, Hablu'l Matin* and *Sur-i Israfil*). While the problems of linguistic reform were already recognized during the 1852-1905 period, even more important efforts included pioneering attempts to analyze the Iranian society and social structure so as to devise a theory of society which could rejuvenate a faltering historiography. (Here one can cite particularly Mirza Aqa Khan Kirmani's works.) The essays of Mirza Fathali Akhundzadeh, and Abdul Rahim Talibuf also contributed considerably to the political discussions of the pre-Constitutional period in recognizing the various classes within Iranian society, the need for educational, legal, and administrative reforms, and the value of scientific research and technology; and, in general, the immediate need for far-reaching reforms in Iran.

By 1905, the Iranian writers and their literature reflected the political struggle of the people through short stories, essays, and poetry. The latter two genre had emerged as the dominant form of communicating the struggle and the courses of action; in fact, poetry had remained the principal form of revolutionary literature through much of Iran's history. It was natural therefore that artists and writers turned to poetry to express the concerns of the people and the courses of action during the Constitutional Period of 1905-1911. The poetry of Muhammad Taqi Bahar illustrates the concerns of the intellectual. In 1909, Bahar wrote in *Kar-i Iran ba Khudast* (The Affairs of Iran Rest with God):

> It is a mistake to talk about freedom with the king
> of Iran, the affairs of Iran rest with God.
> The religion of the king of Iran is different from
> other religions, the affairs of Iran rest with
> God. [3]

On the passing of the Qajars in 1925, he wrote:

Gone is the rule of the Qajars; after sickness came
its death.
Stupidity, indolence, and frivolity have revealed
their hideous end.[4]

Like so many of the Constitutional political leaders and writers, Bahar could understand the tyranny of the Qajar kings but failed to anticipate the autocracy of the Pahlavis.

From 1905 to 1920, therefore, a second important period of contemporary Iran gave rise to experimentations in the literature of politics and struggle, building closely on the works and efforts of the 1852-1905 writers. In addition to Bahar, writers such as Ali Akbar Dihkhuda had begun to compile dictionaries and encyclopedias of new words and ideas to analyze and understand better the changing political realities of the Constitutional Movement. Dihkhuda was also important in expanding his journalistic activities and essay-writing into the older genre of story-telling. Armed with the political issues of reform and constitutional change as well as with the tools of linguistic innovations brought about over the previous two or three decades, Dihkhuda turned to the tale *(qissih, hikayat,* and *dastan)* as a means of reaching a wider audience within Iran.

The publication in 1919 of the pioneering collection of short-stories, *Yeki Bud Va Yeki Nabud* (Once Upon a Time), by Sayyid M. A. Jamalzadeh was a continuation of Dihkhuda's efforts and others to reach a wider public. In his preface, or "manifesto," to Iranian writers, Jamalzadeh makes clear his work is a continuation of previous experimentations in identifying the contradictions within Iranian society and reaching out to the people with the issues of the "democratic" struggle against the king and court. Jamalzadeh stated:

Commonly the very substance of the Iranian political despotism, which is well-known the world over, dominates the matter of literature as well; that is to say, when a writer holds his pen in his hand, his attention is directed solely to the group of the learned and the scholars, and takes no interest whatsoever in the others. He even ignores the many who are fairly literate and can read and comprehend plain, uncomplicated writings quite well.[5]

Jamalzadeh was already calling the attention of the writers of Iran to the issues of the writer's role in society and in politics: for Jamalzadeh, that role was as a "democrat" whose obligations to increase literacy and write in "plain Persian" would facilitate the downfall of the kings and ruling families of the court. His continued publication of short-stories concerning villagers and the "commonfolk" as well as several essays on the social and economic structure of Iran places Jamalzadeh and his predecessor, Ali Akbar Dihkhuda, at the head of the 1905-1920 progressive writers.

In 1919 and 1921, two significant changes occurred in Iran affecting the Iranian people generally and the writers particularly: 1) Britain attempted to establish a protectorate over Iran through the ruling families' approval of the Anglo-Persian Agreement of 1919, thus ensuring British economic and strategic interests in the Gulf and in the Abadan oilfields under the "protective guidance" of the Anglo-Persian Oil Company (APOC), and 2) the *coup d'état* against the Qajars by Sayyid Zia ud-Din Tabataba'i and Reza Khan Pahlavi with the latter assuming one-man rule of Iran in December 1925. The two events inaugurated the third period of Iranian contemporary history, 1921-1941; the period of further exploitation of the villagers, the first labor strikes in the oilfields, and

101

repression of the progressive writers, such as Mirzadeh Ishqi, Abul Qasim Lahuti, and Buzurg Alavi.

Mirzadeh Muhammad Reza Ishqi, born in 1893 in Hamadan, was one of the progressive poets of this period. In his poetry and writings, he described the worsening conditions of Iran and indicated the major external contributory cause:

See the impudence, there is a tumult raging in the West; one says: Persia is mine; the other says: it belongs to us. [6]

In response to Ishqi's vigorous protests against the Anglo-Persian Agreement of 1919, Ishqi was imprisoned in Tehran for a short time only to confront the greater difficulties of the 1921 *coup d'état* and the politics of Reza Khan Pahlavi. In a poem written in 1923, "Ideal-i Ishqi" (Ishqi's Dream), Ishqi revealed his complete opposition to the monarchy and ruling families, calling for revolutionary struggle:

On the day, when the wrath of the nation confronts tyranny, this whole empire will be overthrown. The shy will turn against the traitors of the earth; It will be the time for slaughtering the armies of corpse-washers with whose blood the earth will turn red. [7]

The poem began the comtemporary genre of revolutionary poetry in Iran. In 1924, Ishqi's journal, *Qarn-i Bistom* (The Twentieth Century), was banned. Several days after the banning order was issued, Ishqi was murdered in his house.

Other writers such as Parvin I'tisami, Mirza Abul Qasim Arif, Abul Qasim Lahuti, and Nima Yushij also spoke out in favor of the rights of the urban worker and the villager in opposition to the tyranny of the Qajars and Pahlavis. Parvis I'tisami wrote in the poem, "Sa'iqeh-i Ma

Setam-i Aghniyast" (The Tyranny of the Rich Is a Thunderbolt for Us):

> Humane, just and equalitarian sentiments do not exist
> Because tyranny, oppression, and injustice thrive
> The rights of the worker have been crushed
> Like the grain under the millstone. [8] /

In her *Qalb-i Majruh* (The Wounded Heart), I'tisami comments on the life of the poor through the eyes of a child who wonders why the wealthy children do not want to play with him simply because he is poorly dressed and why they despise him simply because his father is poor.

Abul Qasim Lahuti, another of the progressive writers during the regime of Reza Shah, criticized the deteriorating social and political conditions of Iran of the 1920's:

> From the poverty of the peasant and the tyranny
>   of the landlord, it becomes evident that Iran
>   is being ravaged by despotism and I weep,
> When I see the treacheries of the king and the
>   ignorance of the nation, I fear that the
>   country will collapse and I weep,
> The landlord sells the peasant together with the
>   land and I find that the nation is impotent to
>   prevent this and I weep. [9]

Following an abortive revolt in Tabriz in 1921, Lahuti fled to the Soviet Union and focused on Iran's problems in more obvious Marxist language:

> Death to this world of tyranny and treason which
>   has poor as well as rich, slaves as well as free.
> Long live the hammer and sickle of the toiling
>   masses who will build a new world without
>   classes and contradictions. [10]

And again in these bitter lines:

On this threshold the hilt of the sword as well as the philosophy of religion served as lackeys for the king. The chain of death was fastened to the necks of a hundred beggars so that the king might play with the locks of the beautiful ones. [11]

The vision and themes of Lahuti's poetry rank him as a leader of the revolutionary position in contemporary Iranian literature. His works, like those of Ishqi, are of course, banned in Iran today.

Throughout the two decades of Reza Shah's rule, the modernization in communication and the growth of industry lost much of their potential to improve the lot of the people because of the expropriations of peasants' land, particularly in Mazandaran and Gilan provinces, increased censorship, greater economic and military hardships, and the imprisonment of critics of the regime. The short stories and essays of Jamalzadeh, Sadiq Hidayat, and Buzurg Alavi as well as the poetry of Nima Yushij would accordingly exploit daring and experimental themes and techniques to analyze Iran's social and political problems and structures. Both Hidayat's research into folklore and culture, and Alavi's criticisms of despotism set them apart from the general run during the period 1921-1941. And Buzurg Alavi's works are presently banned in Iran; the author, fleeing imprisonment in the 1940's, has lived in exile since.

From 1941 to 1953, Iran underwent a second "constitutional movement" following the ousting of Reza Khan by the Allies and the placing on the throne of his son, the present king of Iran, Muhammad Reza Pahlavi. The preoccupation with European and Asian campaigns during World War II by the United States and Britain and the rise of another Pahlavi allowed the writers and artists to continue more freely the experiments of 1905-1911.

By 1950, approximately 50 political parties and 150 newspapers thrived in that heady atmosphere of nationalist and reformist activism and parliamentarian politics. In the spring of 1951, Dr. Mossadeq and various members of the *majlis* (Parliament) voted to nationalize the entire Abadan oil field complex, thus setting in motion the final act of British involvement in Iranian society and the withdrawal of American support for the National Front in place of the king and the ruling families. The international oil cartel and American opposition, along with faltering support among the diverse membership of the National Front for Mossadeq's reformist government, finally ended the experimentation of the 1941-1953 period in the "August Days" of 1953. The United States and Britain encouraged the conservatives to overthrow the nationalists (the National Front and the Tudeh) and to reinstate the shah. The efforts of the United States (including the now well publicized intervention of the C.I.A. in Iran's affairs) to terminate the experimentations of the Mossadeq period brought an end to the economic and political independence of the nationalization programs and land reform movements. The gradual replacement of British political and economic support of the Pahlavis by the United States further increased the dependency of the monarchy and its supporters on foreign loans and credits as well as its foreign policies. These August 1953 events were commented on extensively by Iranian writers and artists, both when they occurred and later. The two outstanding writers of the 1941-1953 period, were Jalal Al-i Ahmad and Nima Yushij. While Nima was an active poet in the 1921-1941 period, some of his better poems were to appear later during the "second constitutional" era. The 1942 poem, for example, *Ah, Adamha* (O, Men), foresaw the heroic efforts of Mossadeq in the face of overwhelming odds in the waning hours of August, 1953:

O Men, who sit along the shore and laugh
Someone is drowning in the sea
Someone continues to flay his arms and feet
About the roaring, somber, and ponderous sea.

Someone calls to you from the water
His arms tiring from the fight with the ponderous waves
His mouth open, his eyes wide with terror
He watches your shadows from afar
The azure waters strangle him, each moment
     his terror increases
Sometimes his head, sometimes his foot —
O, Men! [12]

From 1953 to 1957, the poets and short-story writers along with the essayists could publish fewer works in the open, having to resort to allegories and metaphors in order to escape the increased censorship and secret police. The combination of the CIA, British intelligence service, and the powerful families led by General Zahidi swept aside the Mossadeq reforms, crushed the opposition through purges, trials, and imprisonment, and, in 1957, established the SAVAK (Security Organization), principally to control the press and creative writers.

From 1957 to 1963, a number of strikes spread thoughout Iran. Some 20,000 Tehran brickworkers started this period by a strike for increased wages, job security, and benefits. Then, from June to October 1957, the Abadan oil field workers also went on strike again, as they had in 1953, to demand wage increases commensurate with the rise in oil revenues. In April 1958, 12,000 cab drivers in Tehran and other major cities struck to protest the gas hikes and growing general inflation. The June 1959 brickworkers strike with 40,000 participants this time renewed past demands and led to government suppression, leaving 50 dead. The opposition in the towns and cities to the "benign" monarchy culminated in the 21 May, 1961 teachers' strike and the January 1962 military assault on students barricaded in the University of Tehran.

Among the several outstanding poets of this period, including Ahmad Shamlu, Nadir Nadirpur, Nima Yushij, and Mahdi Akhavan Sales, was Siyavush Kasra'i who in 1957 summed up the legacy of August 1953 and the subsequent conflicts with the regime:

It was one day
A dark and distasteful day
Our fortunes blackened by
our oppressors
Our enemy prevailed over our life . . .
And in those days, the significance of bravery was
                                    /buried and
Life itself had meaning only in the arrow
The work of a hundred thousand swords only
                                    /had significance.[13]

In 1961, finally, Jalal Al-i-Ahmad published secretly the first parts of his political essay, *Gharbzadigi* (Westamination), in which he called attention to the poverty of the educational systems as evidence of the decline of Persian culture and society in general:

Great interest in quantity (not quality) still prevails over educational wisdom. And the ultimate goal of "Westaminated" education is the preparation and deposition of documents attesting to the employment value of education in the hands of persons who are able only to become the future clerks of the bureaucracy and who need documents for promotion to any position. There is no coordination in the business of schools. Schools. We have all sorts of them: religious . . . Islamic . . . secular . . . Italian . . .

foreign, and schools that foster spiritual midgets and students of theology. We have technical schools and trade schools, and a legion of other kinds. But nowhere is it entered and recorded what the net result of all this variety is and why all these schools exist and what each of them fosters and for what occupations the products of these schools are being prepared. [14]

All through 1962, the economy continued to falter under rising inflation and the king, along with the ruling families, began to despair over any good results coming from the "liberal" politics of Dr. Amini, the Premier. The planned trip of the king to the United States in April of 1962 was preceded by an unusual outflow of monetary gifts to high-ranking government officials and other personages in Washington and New York. The subsequent Iranian request for further aid from the United States was granted and promises of forthcoming reforms in Iran were extended "to justify" the American largesse. The present era of contemporary Iran was about to begin; that is, the period from 1963 to the present.

The events of June 5-7, 1963 begins the period of Samad Behrangi. On the 5th of June (15 Khurdad 1342), 600 died in the streets of Qum and Tehran. By the end of the following two days, more than 6000 Iranians died in Tehran, Qum, and Mashhad in protest and anger against the regime, the arrest and imprisonment of several religious leaders including Ayatollah Khomeini (now in exile in Najaf, Iraq), and the increased economic, military, and political interests of the United States evidenced through the proclamation of the "White Revolution" in February 1963. The shock of the killings in June 1963, the vain efforts of highly-placed individuals to plead clemency from the king, the politics of the "White Revolution," and the harsh retaliation of the regime finally sounded the death knell to 70 years of parliamentary experimentation, reformist politics, and nationalist activism. Ayatollah Khomeini commented on these events in 1971:

> The monarchy in Iran, from its inception to this day
> – God be my witness – has inflicted miseries and
> perpetuated enormous crimes. The crimes of Persian
> Shahs have blackened the pages of history. Who but
> these very Shahs of Iran ordered massacres of people
> and piled their severed heads into pyramids? The very
> best of these Shahs were ruthless ruffians. [15]

After 1967, the regime had stepped up its "White Revolution," established a number of computerized light-industries to augment the already existing consumer and assembly industries, and agreed with the Soviets to the building of a steel mill in Isfahan in exchange for small weapons purchase and the sale of natural gas. The revenues from light industries compared little, however, to the burgeoning petro-chemical industries' contributions and profits from natural gas exports to Russia. Moreover, most of the new revenues went to the financing of the growing military and SAVAK forces within and outside of Iran. In 1967, Dr. Mossadeq died and, in that year, Forugh Farrukhzad wrote her poem, "Kasi Keh Mesl Hich Kasi Nist" (Someone Like No One Else):

> Someone is coming
> Someone else
> Someone better
> Someone like no one else, not like father, not like
>   Ansee, not like Yahya, not like mother.
>   . . . . .
> and his face
> is more radiant than the face of the twelfth Imam
> and he's not even afraid of Sa'eed Javad himself who
>   owns all the rooms
> in our house

and his name which mother
invokes at the beginning and at the end of her prayers
O, Judge of all Judges
O, Need of all Needs
and he' able
to recite all the difficult words in the Third Grade Book
with his eyes closed
and he's even able
to subtract 1000 from 20 million without anything
       happening
and he's able to get as much as he wants
     from Sa'eed Javad's
     shop
          goods on credit... [16]

Farrokhzad's recitation of a child's yearning for the days
of justice and equality to all including the elimination of
the "1000" families of the ruling regime placed her in the
ranks of the "social" poets of the current period of
literature. After 1967, the government stepped up its
repression of such writers as Gholam Husayn Sa'edi and
Hushang Golshiri through frequent interrogations and
constant harassment of booksellers believed peddlers of
protest literature.

From 1967 to 1969, Samad Behrangi, Gholam
Husayn Sa'edi, Jalal Al-Ahmad, M. Azarm, Khosrow
Golsorkhi, and Fereydoun Tonkaboni took the lead in the
revolutionary current of contemporary Iranian literature.
Each soon paid for such activism in terms of execution or
imprisonment. Asghar Elahi, in his story *Jashn-i Ruz-i
'Ashura* (The Holy Day of Ashura), explains the reaction
of the peasant to the so-called "reforms" of the post-1963
period. In this work, Elahi's peasant discovers the similari-
ties of the *Ta'zieh* or "Passion Play" to his own real village
situation in the depiction of the death of the good Husayn
at the hands of the oppressive Arab rulers (this story being

based on the 7th-century historical events surrounding the death of Ali's son, Husayn, at Karbala, Iraq). The following passage is of particular interest:

> Every year, I would have to fall on the ground and get killed . . . every year, my wife had to fall at the feet of Hajji Mehdi and we had to give our wheat to him. Every year, Shemr (the Arab General who killed Husayn) would kick me in the side, sit on my chest, on my heart, and impale my throat on a spear. Who has said Shemr should always succeed, who has said Shemr and Ibn Sa'd, the Heathen, should kill the Imam Husayn? . . . But I'm killed every year and Ibn Sa'd and Shemr and Yazid succeed. So, corruption and oppression are never eliminated from the earth and the people's condition of life never changes. The oppressors remain, the oppressed are crushed under their feet. They tax us, take the headman's duties, the landlord's duties, tax the land both irrigated and dry and, finally, take the cow. The gendarmerie, the police, the landlord, and the Government all collect tribute. Alas, Imam Husayn doesn't come and the Shemrs and Yazids are legion. [17]

In the end of the story, Elahi's peasant finally decides (to pretend) not to be killed and attacks the oppressor and kills him, saying, "I was very happy . . . at last, Shemr has fallen to the ground and Justice rides on high . . . now I will never lose my sword!"

On 21 March 1969, in answer to the Tehran United Bus Company's fare raise of 100%, the students and urban workers went on strike bringing the bus service in Tehran to a stand-still and eventually led to the burning of a number of buses. In Gilan, protests over the restrictive sale of rice, along with a number of revolts and peasant protests in Kurdistan and Zanjan, resulted in 400 arrests

111

and a number of summary executions. The protests in Kurdistan and West Azarbayjan were related to the suppression of the Kurdish national movement. In June 1969, members of the "Palestine Group" led by Shokrollah Paknejad were arrested. This was a revolutionary group of young Iranians prepared to engage in armed struggle for "the national liberation" of Iran.

The arrival of the 35 American bankers in the summer of 1970 to investigate possible private investment in Iran's domestic economy, the promulgation of the image of a "happy, little kingdom" through international magazines, such as *Time*, and the escalation of attacks on writers and artists, such as Gholam Husayn Sa'edi, Fereydoun Tonkaboni, Sa'id Soltanpur, and M. Azarm were conflicting aspects of the period. The continued censorship and increased repression of civil and human rights were the substance of Shokrollah Paknejad's defense to the military tribunal in December 1970:

> Mr. President, and Gentlemen Judges, are these tortures not shameful in the age of space and conquest of the moon? Yes, you, Gentlemen, will condemn us for having told the truth, but your verdicts will in no way lessen the bitterness of all that has been said, and you know that very well. We are neither the first group to be tried nor the last for having struggled for liberation and against imperialism, in tribunals of the Iranian Army . . . The Iranian Army is run by American and Israeli advisers; the selected officers are sent to USA and Britain for their training; the SAVAK and the Security Branch of the Army are totally run by American advisers. Such an army has no duty but to suppress the liberation movement and independence-seeking elements, to drown in blood any movement that seeks to liberate Iran from under the yoke of the imperialists; this

army has no mission but to arrest, torture, condemn, and execute Iranian freedom-fighters. [18]

On 8 February, 1971, organized armed struggle against the regime and its supporters began in the forests of Gilan province in the region around the village of Siyahkal. Thirteen members of the Iranian People's Fedayeen Guerrillas (OIPFG) were arrested and eight died under torture following several days of combat with the Iranian army. Despite the 2500th Anniversary celebrations organized by the government· in October, 1971, few Iranians appeared to support the regime. Ayatollah Khomeini's statement in Iraq in the Fall of 1971 concerning the celebrations summarizes some of the opposition of the Iranian people to the regime:

Should millions of people's resources be wasted on these base and ridiculous expenditures to celebrate a system of rule that throughout our history has brought shame to us — as it is now doing — with injustice, crime, corruption and prostitution. Just recently he (the king) sent his thugs to ruthlessly beat up students merely because anti-Shah slogans had appeared in the university. As written to me, many women students have had to undergo emergency operations as a result of severe lacerations and wounds inflicted — as well as other criminal assaults which are unmentionable. Their only crime was to show their opposition to these 2500th anniversary celebrations. They said, famine, we do not want you to celebrate over our people's corpses. [19]

In the brief period of 1971 to 1973, 500 Ziba workers went on strike and were attacked by the army. In the same period, 200 Jihan textile workers attempted to march to Tehran to voice protests over the low pay and were also attacked by the army (19 dead and many wounded) while 5000 Isfahan steel workers went on strike for the same reason. In 1972, both Tehran University students and local high school students protested the regime's political and economic alliance with the United States and Europe. The February, 1973 celebration of the 10th Anniversary of the White Revolution (now called the Shah-People Revolution) found few supporters to join in the merrymaking, even in Tehran.

In March 1973, the regime announced a $3-5 billion arms purchase from the United States to be accompanied by 5000-7000 additional American civilian and military personnel. The announcement was met with student strikes and demonstrations in Tehran, Mashhad, Tabriz, and Ahvaz and workers strikes in Tehran. On 3 June 1973, the Iranian People's Combatants (IPCO) attacked and killed an American officer working closely with the Iranian military and police. The escalation of struggle in Tehran was explained in part by Khosrow Golsorkhi in the poem, *Sh'ir-i Binam* (The Untitled Poem):

> Because of your blood,
>> Topkhaneh Square
>>> Will stir to life
>>>> In the wrath of the masses
>
> The People
> From that end of the square will surge over
>> the (north) end:
>
> Bread and hunger
>> Will be divided equitably. [20]

The reference to Topkhaneh Square as a center for conflict is due to its crucial geographical position in Tehran today, located as it is between the wealthy North Tehran districts and the poor South Tehran districts — as well as to the historical importance of the Square as a frequent scene of past uprisings.

From the summer of 1973 to the present, the Government of Iran initiated further exactions on the writers and artists through more arrests, house searches, torture, and executions. In February 1974, Khosrow Golsorkhi was executed for "crimes against the State" and in the February 13, 1975 issue of *The Times,* David Simpson, Director of Amnesty International, British Section, wrote:

> Amnesty International does not generally issue league tables of those countries which, from our worldwide research and legal work, appear to be the worst offenders in violating basic human rights; but, in any such list, whether of torture, of executions after sham trials, or of extensive political imprisonment, Iran would be a world leader.[21]

The rise in the number of political prisoners, which is said to be 40,000, and further Iranian involvement in Gulf politics, including the Dhofari revolution against Oman, indicates the present government's intentions to continue its policies of the past.

Thus, the historical stages of the conflict between the poor rural and urban communities of Iran and the "loving king of kings" plus the ruling families have delineated the stages of literary and political changes:

1852-1905: rise of intellectuals and developments in journalism, essay-writing, and historiography.

1905-1921: Constitutional Movement and the short-story form; the clearer polarization of revolutionary and reformist writers and artists.

1921-1941: rise in British influence and Pahlavis along with new interests in revolutionary poetry, folklore, and the short story.

1941-1953: "Second Constitutional Movement" with further polarization of the writers and political parties; the use of essays and journals is improved upon.

1953-1957: rise in American influence and Pahlavis restored; the publication of the "little magazines" and importance of poetry for the writers.

1957-1963: relaxation of some political experimentation under SAVAK's care, the uneasy economic conditions, and publication of *Gharbzadigi* secretly.

1963 to present: collapse of the reformist politics, rise of organized armed struggle, and blossoming of revolutionary literature.

It is in the context of the historical progression of worsening socio-economic and political conditions in Iran that we can begin to analyze Samad Behrangi's works and thoughts. It is evident that the obstacles to change in Iran's contemporary history, such as the continued existence of a semi-feudal and semi-capitalist society under the domination of the king and ruling families, had to concern Behrangi as a writer and observer and educator of contemporary Iran.

Indeed, Samad Behrangi concerned himself with the obstacles to change within Iran. Furthermore, he sought to clarify the social and political contradictions in Iranian society both past and present as well as to invite his readers and Iranians to consider alternatives to the society. Finally, Behrangi illustrated through his works the means necessary to remove the present obstacles; that is, the action needed to change the society. To Behrangi, the necessary action was revolutionary struggle. Indeed, Samad Behrangi was himself the artist in revolutionary struggle.

II.

Let them torture me, let them sacrifice my flesh and blood on behalf of the masses — as long as there is

116

oppression, there will be struggle; as long as there is struggle, there will be defeats and victories with the (final) victory going to the masses. I don't make this claim, history does.[22]

The words of Mehdi Reza'i before the military tribunal in his 1973 trial articulates the feelings of a growing number of Iranian people towards their government. Samad Behrangi raised the same issues in his children's literature.

In the Introduction to the "Bald Pigeon Keeper," Behrangi admonishes his readers:

You must ask a thousand other questions to understand society and its problems. Remember that society is not contained within the four walls of your homes. Society includes all places where our fellow countrymen live . . . All of this is the society you will inherit from your fathers. But you must not pass this inheritance untouched on to your own children. You must reduce its ills and eliminate problems, increase its strong points, and find medicine for its diseases and eventually eradicate them.[23]

From the five stories included in the present collection, three important themes emerge: 1) the vibrant culture of the Iranian peoples, and the historical conflict between the monarchy plus ruling families and the revolutionary groups; 2) the importance of education and the need to integrate and inter-relate culture and history with a more rational, less traditional view of society; 3) the need for armed struggle in order to create lasting benefits for all the people—not just for the privileged few.

For Behrangi, the culture (history, religion, languages, literatures, and arts) and the people are inseparable; the former arose out of the latter. Thus, an attack against Iranian culture was an attack against the Iranian peoples

117

themselves; that is, either against their religion, languages, literatures, or history. Through his research into folklore and culture (a continuity of the earlier work of Sadiq Hidayat, Jalal Al-i Ahmad, and Gholam Husayn Sa'edi, and his eleven years in Azarbayjani villages, Behrangi discovered the aspirations of the Azarbayjani rural communities and strove to preserve the culture through his short stories and translations. In doing so, he intended to lay the foundation for his analysis of Azarbayjani and Iranian society; that is, he intended to build a theory of society based on his years as a teacher and his intimate knowledge of the villages of Iran.

The two short stories, "The Bald Pigeon Keeper" and "The Little Sugar Beet Vendor," well illustrate Behrangi's consciousness of the culture and politics of Iranian villagers. In both stories, two levels of conflict between the workshop owners (Hajji Qoli and Hajji Ali) and the peasants (Tarvardi and the Pigeon Keeper) on the one hand and the armed supporters of the property owners (the headman and the king) and the peasants on the other highlight the basic contradictory positions and interests of the peasant and the upper classes in Iranian society. The peasant's major concern to survive through labor on the land and in the workshops is directly hindered and limited by the workshop owners' principal concern for profit and benefits (the differential in the town-village salaries in "The Little Sugar Beet Vendor," the profits of Hajji Ali in "The Bald Pigeon Keeper,") is emphasized. The role of the police, village headman, king, and army in enforcing and insuring the growth of profits, the enrichment of the upper classes and the exploitative economic and sexual relations between Hajji Qoli and Tarvardi's sister and other village women are also scored.

In contrast, just and equitable relations occur as a direct result of full participation of the society in the labor force and survival of that society (the princess in "The

Bald Pigeon Keeper" is told she must work for her living, Tarvardi and his sister work for her dowry rather than accept the bribes of Hajji Qoli, and Kachal's duty to return Hajji Ali's property to the rightful owners, that is, the villagers and urban laborers). Despite the admonitions of Hajji Qoli to Tarvardi ("It's not for you or your mother to like or dislike") regarding the buying of Tarvardi's sister, or the open threats of police action and loss of job in the rug workshop, Tarvardi embraced armed struggle as his only means of protecting his sister's honor and his family's name.

The Pigeon Keeper also resorted to armed struggle as a result of his relationship to Hajji Ali and the king; a relationship which was more in the Iranian tradition of the *pahlavan* or people's hero and protector. In the Pigeon Keeper's case, the resistance was not temporary but continuous; again, a characteristic of the district hero found in other contemporary Persian short stories, such as the hero of Sadiq Hidayat's "Dash Akul."

Finally, the description of the living conditions of Tarvardi's hut, the village, and the school as well as the Pigeon Keeper's hovel, particularly in contrast to the conditions of the wealthy, shows the stark reality of poverty and oppression so frequently found in contemporary Iran. Despite the efforts of the present regime to mask over "those realities" through glossy travelogues and colorful panoramic publications, the realism of Behrangi's stories is compelling and, to the perceptive observer of Iran, accurate.

The second and third themes of Behrangi's literature are in the three remaining stories, "One Peach - A Thousand Peaches," "The Little Black Fish," and "24 Restless Hours"; that is, "the importance of a scientific and rational view of history, culture, and society obtained through observation, experience, and acquaintance with Iranian society and culture. Here more than in the two

119

other stories, Behrangi emphasizes the great contrasts between the social classes and the deep contradictions of the society which generate the exploitative and oppressive conditions so obvious in contemporary Iran.

In "The Little Black Fish," an allegorical tale of the ways to achieve knowledge and consciousness of the dynamics of society, Behrangi raises basic questions concerning change and continuity in life and builds a clear understanding of society through the experiences of others. The initial departure of the little black fish (from his mother's home) and the resulting uproar due to the fish's desire "to see the end of the stream" is a very important lesson in education and politics. The more the fish was pressed by his mother and neighbors to stay, the clearer the issues became. When questioned as to how the fish learned about there being "another world" and "an end to the stream", anyway, the fish replied he learned about these matters on his own and from listening to others. After enduring the constant complaints of the old fishes, the little black fish wanted to know "is there another way to live in the world?"; a question the little fish could not answer until he had traveled and experienced other "worlds."

Once embarked on the long trip to the sea, the fish encountered both valuable friends (the lizard who armed the fish with a sword) and instructive enemies (the pelican, the frog, and the heron). Through the succession of encounters and experiences along the way, the fish expanded his knowledge of the world and methods of survival. Upon reaching the sea and meeting other fish who had also traveled to the sea, the little black fish finally was content and could answer the question about living another way in the world with confidence and clarity. While basking in the sea, the fish states:

. . . if someday I should be forced to face death—as I

shall—it doesn't matter. What does matter is the influence that my life or death will have on the lives of others . . .[24]

The allegory ends with the little black fish setting out to kill the heron who oppresses the others, only to die himself in the ensuing death-struggle. But the story is not over:

Eleven thousand, nine hundred and ninety-nine little fish said good night and went to sleep. The grand-mother fell asleep, too. But try as she might, a little red fish just couldn't get to sleep. All night long she thought about the sea . . . [25]

The story "One Peach - A Thousand Peaches" is a beautiful recitation of the peasant-landlord conflict in Iran from the viewpoint of a peach seed, nurtured and cultivated by two peasant boys, Poulad and Saheb Ali. Immediately, the reader learns of the unjust ways land is divided between the landlord and peasants "following recent reforms" (meaning the "White Revolution") as well as the unfair distribution of the products of the land (the gardener takes all the peaches to the landlord in the town). The fact that not one peach is left for the villagers "as if we weren't human" according to Poulad, forces Poulad and Saheb Ali to raid the orchard which stands on village land. The gardener, armed to protect the landlord's orchard from the peasants, resembles the headman in "The Little Sugar-Beet Vendor" whose role is to enforce the landlord's oppression and illegal seizure of the products of the land. Because the peach does not want to be wasted on the landlord's daughter who takes one or two bites and throws the peach away (as well as receiving fruit flown in from foreign lands), the peach longs to be eaten by the two hungry boys. When it is eaten and its seed then returned and planted in the orchard by Poulad and Saheb

121

Ali, Behrangi carefully details the growth of the seed into a healthy peach tree at the hands of the two villagers.

The importance of careful planning and preparedness ("strong veins and roots in the ground") before emerging to begin service to others (the peach dreams of feeding half-naked peasant children only) is Behrangi's invitation to study and education for political action. Throughout the story, Behrangi details the dialectics of society, the scientific process of change, and the interaction of causes and effects. The story, ending with the death of Saheb Ali (who died so that the peach tree might live) and the departure of Poulad to the town, is a fine example of Behrangi's manifesto to his countrymen, children and adults alike; the manifesto to research the problems of society, raise one's political consciousness, and prepare for action.

In "24 Restless Hours," Behrangi delineates the social conflicts and the inevitability of armed struggle, thus continuing his position as a revolutionary artist in contemporary Iranian politics. The story of Latif in Tehran as part of the urban poor driven to the towns and cities by the conditions of the villages is a moving account of the gulf dividing the rich and poor in Tehran and Iran today.

Characteristically, the story's important dialogues occur between Latif and the toy animals, particularly the camel. As in another Behrangi story, "Olduz and The Talking Doll," the camel guides Latif through the basic lessons in the contradictions of Iranian society, explaining the meaning of poverty and wealth through the word "villa" and contrasting the rich and clean North Tehran region with the poor and filthy South Tehran districts; a contrast found in Khosrow Golsorkhi's imagery of Topkhaneh Square in the previously cited "The Untitled Poem."

Latif's desire to buy the toy camel and thereby

befriend his faithful guide forever is thwarted by his meager earnings as a street urchin. Nonetheless, his determination to possess the intelligent and instructive camel never flags until the end. In the waning hours of his stay in Tehran, Latif learns that money *is* available but of course only to the few. With the new insights into the conditions of villagers and his father's condition, and knowledge of the contradictions between villagers and the Tehrani rich, Latif desperately attempts to keep the camel from the well-dressed little girl whose father bought the toy. As he watches the car and camel disappear into the Tehran traffic, Latif "wished only he owned the machine gun in the store window." In the end, Latif was prepared for armed struggle.

Samad Benrangi is thus both artist and revolutionary as evidenced by his own life and works. The importance of children's stories in the educational and political effort to influence both the children and adults of Iran is due to their direct and simple language, and their greater opportunities to evade censorship through allegories and metaphors. It is therefore no coincidence that children's literature became one of the most important genres of post-June 1963 Iran. In his Introduction to "Olduz and The Talking Doll," Behrangi has the Talking Doll state:

. . . every pampered and selfish child has no right to read Olduz and my story, particularly the wealthy children who ride in big cars, look cocky, and think they're heads taller than the vagabond and raggedy children in the street, never passing through the working-class districts. Mr. Behrangi himself said he writes principally for the vagabond, raggedy working-class children. Of course, misguided and self-indulgent children can read Mr. Behrangi's stories but only after correcting their thoughts and actions. [26]

The words are reminiscent of Parvin I'tisami's poem,

Qalb-i Majruh (The Wounded Heart), previously cited.

For Fereydoun Tonkaboni, as for most contemporary Iranian writers, the literature of Iran must come alive and explain the society in all its contradictions. In Tonkaboni's *Anduh-i Satarvan Budan* (The Sorrow of Infertility), he explains:

> We don't need a book which puts the reader to sleep with a full stomach in a plush chair near a warm pot-belly stove in the winter, or in an air-conditioned room in the summer. Rather, we need a book which the reader hides in his pocket and walks through the street trembling from fear of its discovery! [27]

In the course of explaining the need for a new kind of children's literature, Behrangi stated his position clearly, noting the need to present literature differently from the sort provided in the First Grade Persian reader:

> The time of limiting children's literature to passive propaganda and rigid, fruitless institutions has ended. We must lead our children away from building hopes on false and empty visions towards creating hopes based on a correct understanding and interpretation of the harsh realities of the society and on how to struggle to eliminate those harsh realities. [28]

Samad Behrangi, then, did not limit himself to veiled allegories and masked protest only. He was a totally involved revolutionary artist.

FOOTNOTES:

1. *Farsi: Baray-i Kelas-i Avval-i Dabestan* (Persian: First Grade Elementary School), (Tehran, 1346/1967), p. 87. The translation is by this writer.

2. Muhammad Reza Pahlavi, *The White Revolution*, (Tehran, n.d.), p. 2.

3. Muhammad Taqi Bahar, "Kār-i Iran ba Khudast (The Affairs of Persia Rest with God)," in *Post-Revolution Persian Verse* by Munibar Rahman, (Aligarh, 1955), pp. 25-26.

4. *Idem*, in *Post-Revolution Persian Verse* by Munibar Rahman, p. 29.

5. Muhammad Ali Jamalzadeh in "The Shaping of the Modern Persian Short Story: Jamalzadih's 'preface' to *Yiki Bud, Yiki Nabud*," by Haideh Daragahi in *Literary Review*. XVIII, pt. 1 (Fall, 1974), p. 24.

6. Muhammad Reza Ishqi in "Rastākhīz (Resurrection)," in *Post-Revolution Persian Verse* by Munibar Rahman, p. 67.

7. *Idem*, "Ideal-i Ishqi (Ishqi's Dream)," in *Post-Revolution*, pp. 70-71.

8. Parvin I'tisami in "Sa'iqeh-i Ma Setam-i Aghniyast (The Tyranny of the Rich is a Thunderbolt for Us)," in *Post-Revolution*, pp. 78-79. The translation is by this writer.

9. Abul Qasim Lahuti in *Post-Revolution*, p. 44.

10. *Idem* in *Post-Revolution*, p. 45.

11. *Idem* in *Post-Revolution*, pp. 49-50.

12. Nima Yushij, "Ay, Adamha (O, Men)," in *La litterature de l'Iran contemporain*, II by F. Machalski (Warsaw, 1967), p. 176. The translation is by this writer.

13. Siavush Kasra'i, "Aresh-i Kamangir (The Meaning of the Archer)," in the article "Tahlili az Adabiyat-i Mobaraz-i Mo'asir-i Iran (An Analysis of Revolutionary Literature of Contemporary Iran)," *Danishju*, XX, pt. 2 (Azar, 1352/1973), p. 46. The translation is by this writer.

14. Jalal Al-i Ahmad, "Farhang va Danishgah Cheh Mikonand?(What Are Culture and the University Doing)," in *Gharbzadigi*, Chapter IX, (Tehran, 1341/1962), pp. 94-95. The translation is by this writer.

15. Ayatollah Khomeini, "A Religious Leader Speaks Out...," *Iran Report*, (Autumn, 1971), p. 1.

16. Forugh Farrukhzad, "Two Poems: One Window and Someone like no one else (translated by Thomas M. Ricks)," *Literary Review*, XVIII, pt. 1 (Fall, 1974), p. 107.

17. Asghar Elahi in "Tahlili az Adabiyat-i Mobaraz (An Analysis of Revolutionary Literature)," p. 48. The translation is by this writer.

18. Shokrollah Paknejad, *The "Palestine Group" Defends Itself in Military Tribunal*, (Tehran, 1970), pp. 29-30.

125

19. Khomeini, "A Religious Leader Speaks Out . . . ,"p. 1.

20. Khosrow Golsorkhi, "Sh'ir-i Binam (The Untitled Poem)," in *Majmu'ehi az Asar-i Khosrow Golsorkhi,* (Tehran, 1353/1974), p. 91. The translation is by this writer.

21. David Simpson, "Human Rights in Iran," *The Times,* Thursday 13 February 1975.

22. "Mehdi Reza'i dar Bidadgah-i Rezhim (Mehdi Reza'i Before the Court of Injustice of the Regime)," in a newsletter of the Iranian Students Association in Chicago, (Chicago, n.d.). The translation is by this writer.

23. Samad Behrangi, "Chand Kalameh (Some Words)," Introduction to *Kachal-i Kaftarbaz* (The Bald Pigeon Keeper) in *The Little Black Fish and Other Stories* translated by Mary and Eric Hooglund, (Washington, D.C., 1976), p. 78.

24. *Idem,* "Mahi Siyah-i Kuchulu (The Little Black Fish)," in this translation of *The Little Black Fish And Other Stories,* translated by Mary and Eric Hooglund, p. 16.

25. *Ibid.,* p.19.

26. *Idem,* "Chand Kalameh (Some Words)," Introduction to *Olduz va Arusak-i Sokhangu* (Olduz and The Talking Doll), p. 4. The translation is by this writer.

27. Fereydoun Tonkaboni in "Tahlili az Adabiyat-i Mobaraz (An Analysis of Revolutionary Literature)," p. 49. The translation is by this writer.

28. "Introduction," in *The Little Black Fish And Other Stories By Samad Behrangi,* translated from Persian by the Iranian Students Association, (California, 1972), p. ii.

Bibliography

compiled by Thomas Ricks

Bibliography of sources of Samad Behrangi and contemporary Iran used in the present essay:

I. Selected Works in Persian by Samad Behrangi:

A. Short Stories
   Afsaneh-i Mohabat (The Love Story), Winter, 1346/1967.
   Bist-o-Chahar Sa'at dar Khab va Bidari (24 Restless Hours).
      Spring, 1348/1969.
   Kachal-i Kaftarbaz (The Bald Pigeon Keeper). Fall,
      1346/1967.
   Koroughlu va Kachal-i Hamzeh (The Son of a Blind Man and
      Bald Hamzeh). Spring, 1348/1969.
   Mahi Siyah-i Kuchulu (The Little Black Fish). Summer,
      1347/1968.
   Olduz va Arusak-i Sokhangu (Olduz and The Talking Doll).
      Fall, 1346/1967.
   Olduz va Kalagh'ha (Olduz and The Crows). Fall,
      1345/1966.
   Pesarak-i Labuforush (The Little Sugar-Beet Vendor). Fall,
      1346/1967.
   Talkhun va Chand Qissih-i Digar (Talkhun and Some Other
      Stories). n.d.
   Yek Holu, Hezar Holu (One Peach, A Thousand Peaches).
      Spring, 1348/1969.

127

B. Essays

Kandokav dar Masa'il-i Tarbiyati-yi Iran (Investigations into the Educational Problems of Iran). Summer, 1344/1965.
Majmu'eh-yi Maqaleh'ha (Collection of Articles). Summer, 1348/1969.

C. Folklore and Poems

Afsaneh'ha-yi Azarbayjan (Tales of Azarbayjan), translated from Turkish into Persian. 2 vols. Spring, 1344 and 1347/1965 and 1968.
Pareh Pareh (Tiny Pieces). Summer, 1342/1963.

D. Translations

Daftar-i Asha'ir-i Mu'asir az Chand Sha'ir-i Farsi Zaban (A Notebook of Contemporary Poems from Some Persian Poets). n.d.
Kalagh Siyaheh (The Crow). Summer, 1348/1969.
Kharabkar: Qissih'ha-yi az Chand Navisandeh-i Turk Zaban (Saboteur: Stories from Some Turkish Writers). Summer, 1348/1969.

II. Selected Works in Persian and English on Samad Behrangi and Contemporary Persian Literature:

Azarm, M. *Paygah-i Sh'ivi (the Stages of Poetry)*. Tehran, n.d.
"Darbarey-i Samad Behrangi (Concerning Samad Behrangi)," *Aresh*, II, pt. 5, no. 18 (Azar, 1347/November-December, 1968), Special Issue by the Writers Association of Iran.
"Darbarey-i Samad (Concerning Samad)," in *Daneshjoo*, XXI, Pt. 1 (Fall, 1351/1972), pp. 4-11.
Golsorkhi, Khosrow. "People and the Helplessness of Plunderers." *Iran Report*, II (February, 1975), pp. 8-12.
———. "Politics of Art and Poem." *Iran Report*, I (September, 1974), pp. 25-27.
Hezarkhani, Manuchehr. "Jehanbini-yi Mahi Siyah-i Kuchulu (The World-View of The Little Black Fish)." *Aresh*, II, pt. 5, no. 18 (Azar, 1347/November-December, 1968), pp. 17-29.
"Iranian Culture and Art Suppressed," *Resistance: A Quarterly English Defense Publication of the Iranian Students Association in the United States*, II, pt. 3 (April, 1974), pp. 1-5.
Kamshad, Hassan. *Modern Persian Prose Literature*. Cambridge, 1966.

The Little Black Fish and Other Stories by Samad Behrangi.
Translated from Persian by the Iranian Student Association
in the United States. California, 1972.

Majmu'ehi az Asar-i Khosrow Golsorkhi (A Collection of Works
of Khosrow Golsorkhi). World Confederation of Iranian
Students. Khrudad, 1353/June-July, 1974.

Majmu'ehi az Asar-i Samad Behrangi (A Collection of Works of
Samad Behrangi). World Confederation of Iranian Students.
Azar, 1348/November-December, 1969.

"On Some Aspects of Iranian Arts." *Iran Report,* III (May,
1975), pp. 8-12.

Rahman, Munibar. *Post-Revolution Persian Verse.* Aligarh, 1955.

Ricks, Thomas M., ed. "Iran: Contemporary Persian Literature."
Literary Review, XVIII, pt. 1 (Fall, 1974). Special Issue.

Rypka, Jan *et al. History of Iranian Literature.* Dordrecht,
Holland, 1967.

"Tahlil va Tafsiri dar Qissih-i Kachal-i Kaftarbaz (Analysis and
Commentary on the Story of The Bald Pigeon Keeper)."
Bihrang, II (Farvardin, 1352/March-April, 1973), pp. 2-12.

"Tahlili az Adabiyat-i Mobaraz-i Mo'asir-i Iran (An Analysis of
the Revolutionary Literature of Contemporary Iran)." *Danishju,* XXII, pt. 2 (Azar, 1352/November-December, 1973),
pp. 42-49.

Tolu': Taqvim beh Honarmandan-i Mobaraz-i Dar Band (Rising:
An Evaluation of Revolutionary Artists in Captivity). Iranian
Students Association in the United States. Fall, 1352/1973.

Yar-Shater, Ehsan. "Persian Letters in the Last Fifty Years."
Middle Eastern Affairs, XI, pt. 10 (November, 1960), pp.
298-306.

III. Selected Works on Contemporary Iran:

Armajani, Yahya. *Iran.* Englewood Cliffs, New Jersey, 1972.

Avery, Peter. *Modern Iran.* 2nd Edition. London, 1967.

Azadeh, Behrouze, "L'Iran Aujourd'hui." *Le Temps Modernes,*
XXVII, pt. 298 (Mai, 1971), pp. 2031-2066.

Banani, Amin. *The Modernization of Iran, 1921-1941.* Stanford,
California, 1961.

Bill, James A. *The Politics of Iran.* Columbus, Ohio, 1972.

Cook, Fred. "The Billion-Dollar Mystery: A Documented
Thriller Involving American Foreign Aid, the Shah of Iran, a
Desert Chieftain, Swiss Banks, Tapped Wires, Secret Diplo-

macy and Some Celebrated Americans." *The Nation,* CC, pt. 15 (12 April 1965), pp. 380-397.

Cottam, Richard W. *Nationalism in Iran.* Pittsburgh, 1964.

"Iran: The People's Struggle." Iranian Students Association. Chicago, n.d.

"Iran: 20 Years After the CIA Coup." *Iran Report,* I (September, 1973).

"Iranian People's Movement: 1953-1973." *Iran Report,* II (June, 1974), pp. 1-42.

"Iranian Women: Oppression and Struggle." *Resistance,* I, pt. 4 (June, 1973), pp. 7-13.

"Iranian Workers: Life and Struggle." *Resistance,* I, pt. 5 (July, 1973), pp. 1-9.

Jandaghi, Ali. "The Present Situation in Iran." *Monthly Review* (November, 1973), pp. 34-47.

Lambton, A.K.S. *The Persian Land Reform.* Oxford, 1969.

"More About Torture in Iran." *Iran Report,* (February, 1975), pp. 13-18.

Nirumand, Bahman. *Iran: The New Imperialism in Action.* New York, 1969.

"Nixon Doctrine in the Persian Gulf." *Resistance,* I, pt. 2 (April, 1973), pp. 16-18.

Paine, C. and Schoenberger, E. "Iranian Nationalism and The Great Powers: 1872-1954." *MERIP Reports,* No. 37 (May, 1975), pp. 3-10.

"Persian Gulf and Iran's Military Build-Up." *Iran Report,* (February, 1975), pp. 3-7.

Paknejad, Shokrollah. *The 'Palestine Group' Defends Itself in Military Tribunal.* Iran Report Special Issue. Florence, Italy, 1971.

"Repression: Shah's Weapon Inside/Outside Iran." *Resistance,* II, pt. 2 (November, 1973), pp. 4-7.

"A Religious Leader Speaks Out . . ." *Iran Report* (Autumn, 1971), pp. 1-2.

Rey, Lucien. "Persia in Perspective," *New Left Review,* nos. 19 and 20 (1963), pp. 32-55 and 69-98.

Richards, Helmut. "America's Shah, Shahanshah's Iran." *MERIP Reports,* No. 40 (October, 1975), pp. 3-22.

"System of Injustice, I." *Resistance,* I, pt. 2 (April, 1973), pp. 4-9.

"System of Injustice, II." *Resistance,* I, pt. 4 (June, 1973), pp. 14-21.

"Superpower Contention in the Persian Gulf." *Iran Report* (September, 1974), pp. 2-6.

"Torture in Iran." *Iran Report* (September, 1974), pp. 7-20.

"US-Shah Increase Military Ties." *Resistance*, I, pt. 2 (April, 1973), pp. 10-12.

Yar-Shater, Eshan, ed. *Iran Faces the Seventies*. New York, 1971.

Zabih, Sepehr. *The Communist Movement in Iran*. Berkeley, 1966.

Zonis, Marvin. *The Political Elite in Iran*. Cambridge, Mass., 1971.

Notes on Translators
and
Bibliographic Essayist

Mary Elaine Hooglund (b. 1944) took her B.A. at Augustana College, Sioux Falls, South Dakota and her M.A. in anthropology at New York University. She has studied at many other institutions, including Goethe Institute, Kochel-am-See, West Germany, and is presently completing a docotorate at SUNY in Binghamtom, New York. She served in the Peace Corps in Iran and speaks, reads, and writes Persian and Arabic. **Eric Hooglund** (b. 1944), also a former Peace Corps volunteer in Iran, has been a Researcher at the Woodrow Wilson International Center for Scholars, a Fulbright-Hays Research Fellow in Iran, and has taken a doctorate at Johns Hopkins in international relations with Middle East specialty, and currently works with the Carnegie Endowment for International Peace. He is fluent in Persian.

Dr. Thomas Ricks, writer of the Bibliographical-Historical Essay in this volume, has written many articles on Persian history and literature and was the editor of the special issue "Iran" of the *Literary Review* (Vol. XVIII, No. 1, Fall 1974). He teaches African History and Middle Eastern History at Georgetown University, Washington, D.C., and is a former Peace Corps volunteer and research scholar in Iran. He is fluent in Persian and has translated "The Little Black Fish" and other Iranian works published in leading journals.